I0591436

Metaphorosis

November 2022

Beautifully made speculative fiction

Also from Metaphorosis

Metaphorosis

November 2022

edited by
B. Morris Allen

ISSN: 2573-136X (online)
ISBN: 978-1-64076-240-4 (e-book)
ISBN: 978-1-64076-241-1 (paperback)

Metaphorosis
a magazine of speculative fiction
from
Metaphorosis Publishing

Neskowin

November 2022

If Gold Runs Red

Gordon Grice

"Thirteen's too old to be scared of a rock," Clay's dad smirked, even though Clay hadn't said he was scared. They'd come to fish beneath a huge outcrop that loomed over the creek like a giant bending to drink. Hollows brimming with bird droppings glared down at them. Flecks of gleaming green mineral pocked its gray face. Fifty feet up, sage grass and brambles jutted from its crown.

"Remember how I told you," Dad said. "The hook goes through three times, but leave enough worm loose to thrash around and draw some attention."

"Yes, sir," Clay said. They settled down on a lichen-crusted boulder. Clay imagined threading a huge hook three times through Dad. *Leave enough of me loose to thrash around and draw some attention,* Dad would no doubt say, as if he ever failed to draw attention to himself.

"What are you giggling about?" Dad barked. "You'll scare the fish."

Clay sat quietly then. His line looked bent where it entered the water. Six feet down, catfish groped dreamily among the water plants.

Something splashed downstream. Clay glimpsed a bulbous form sliding into the creek.

"We'll have to hunt those beavers out," Dad said. "Look at all those lodges." Clay looked. He had seen the unruly stacks of twigs when they hiked in to look over their new farm, but he hadn't realized what they were. Back east, they never saw beavers. "There's half a dozen dams, too," Dad went on. "That's what slows the creek down and makes this whole area swampy. Clear them out and we'll have a good five acres more to farm."

"Oh," Clay said. Farm work didn't interest him much; he would have preferred to look at the catfish in their dreamy depths.

"Well, I'll be!" Dad shouted, pulling in his line. A fish thrashed at the end of it, paused, then thrashed again. Dad landed it on the boulder and crouched over it. "My God!" he whispered. It was ugly as a sock full of mud, with isinglass eyes glaring over a gaping mouth surrounded by wormy tendrils. As it thrashed, it got its legs under it. It had, by Clay's count, five—jointed, wiry legs like a crawdad's. It went scampering toward the water, and Dad yanked the line to bring it back. "Give me your knife," he said, and Clay unfolded it and held it out to him. "Handle first, dumbass," Dad said. It seemed a shame to kill the fish; it might be the only one of its sort in the world. After Dad gutted it, the fish still struggled feebly to remove the hook, grasping at it with tiny fingers on the end of its tendrils. Dad eased the hook out and dropped the fish into the bucket, which Mama had pointlessly scoured before they set out. Clay hoped its misery was over, but then he heard its little hands—there was no other word for them—scratching at the tin walls.

The next fish they caught was a wonder. It had bigger hands, but only a few wispy legs, hardly enough to scamper on.

Half a dozen ugly fish later, they trudged home along the creek. Clay suddenly raised his eyes to a line of elms fussing in the wind. Some other sound had mingled in with the fussing. Listened for, it went unheard. The elms paused as if to show they had nothing to hide. They stood still as the purple hills beyond. Then a breeze rattled them into motion again.

Clay set down his pole and the bucket full of strange fish and went looking. Dad lumbered on ahead, eyes on the ground, lost in his own thoughts. With luck, Clay could catch up before Dad noticed his absence. The strange sound resumed, subsided, leapt forth once more. Maybe it was water shouldering through stubborn reeds. It might almost have been the weeping of a child. Clay ventured onto stones slick with creek-moss. At last, beneath a cottonwood whose leaves winked and glittered in the wind, he glimpsed bright red and, a second later, a yellow brighter than that.

"Looks like an owl nearly got him, or an eagle," said a grizzled man Clay hadn't noticed. The crooked twig of oak in his hand looked too flimsy to fish with, but the legged catfish dangling from its tip said otherwise.

"What kind of a bird is it?" Clay said. The bright shape flipped and shivered. Its feathers were yellow but stained with welling blood.

"I see you caught one of these deformed fish too," Dad said, interrupting the old man's answer. His boots sent river-rocks clattering out of his way.

"Skitterfish, they call them," the old man said. "My name's Hawkins."

"Ours is Brown," Dad said. Clay could see he was trying his trick of squeezing just a little too hard on the handshake 'to let the other fellow know who's boss'. Hawkins winced, but never stopped smiling. "Skitterfish, you say?"

"Good eating," Hawkins said. "A little butter if you have it, a little salt. People catch them all along this stretch."

"That will have to stop," Dad said. "This land is mine now."

"Folks are used to open range around here," Hawkins smiled. "Cattle country, you know."

"That will have to stop," Dad repeated.

The bird shrilled. Kneeling over it, Clay saw brown ants nibbling its wounds. He brushed them away, like sand from silk. It cooed.

"You'll see lots of strange animals along Saxum Creek," Hawkins said to Clay, as if he had lost interest in Dad. "Too many legs, too smart, too hard to kill. I've seen beaver lodges built with labyrinths inside, like some architect had laid them out. I've seen eagles smart enough to pull the hook out of a fish and fly off with it. I've taken the trophy head from a ten-point buck, only to see the body wander off before I could butcher it. They say it's the saxum —that's the mineral that washes out of that Great Saxum Rock where you were fishing." He pulled a nugget from his pocket, like lead peppered with chips of malachite.

Just then they heard a staccato slapping. Again Clay only glimpsed the beavers slipping into the creek—two of them this time, each leaving a wake of ripples to show where it swam below.

"I'll have to hunt those damn beavers out," Dad said.

"Worth a try," Hawkins said, his smile withering almost into a sneer. "You might look up Hal Vinson in town. He's a trapper from way back."

All the way home, with a pole over his shoulder and the handle of the heavy bucket cutting into his right hand, Clay felt the bird softly thrashing in the bib of his overalls, bumping the little nugget of saxum Hawkins had given him.

"Clay and I've plotted the lodges along my whole property, and the dams too," Dad said, leaning over the hand-drawn map he'd spread on the kitchen table.

"That's a pretty good map," Hal Vinson mumbled. He winced shyly as Mama refilled his coffee. He was a taciturn man, more mustache than meat, and his red eyes looked perpetually on the verge of weeping. Dad said that meant he was a drunk.

"My boy's good at drawing," Dad said. Clay was glad he wasn't at the table where he'd have to acknowledge the compliment. He sat on the floor fixing up a box for the bird he'd brought home, pretending not to hear them. "Point is, how to remove them. Dynamite?"

"Ruin your fishing that way," Vinson mumbled, softer than before, as if to mute a criticism. "I'd say hitch a mule to them and pull. But them beavers are mean. Have to shoot them first."

"I never heard of a mean beaver. How much for the whole job?"

Vinson blinked his bleary eyes. Clearly he wanted no part of such a job.

"I'll give you the pelts," Dad said. "Any beaver pelt you take on my land, by gun or trap, is yours."

Vinson twitched visibly. It was clear to Clay that this represented a greater sum than Dad realized, which Vinson nonetheless preferred to decline. But he withered under Dad's gaze.

"I'll do it for the pelts, I guess," he blinked.

In the night, Clay woke to weeping. The helpless bird showed yellow in the moonlight. When he lit a candle he saw mosquitoes crouching to kiss its wounds. Their bellies swelled so full he saw the vermillion within. The bird writhed and cried.

"Shut that damn bird up!" Dad's voice thundered from the other bedroom, and then Mama's said something soothing that Clay couldn't make out.

He brushed the mosquitoes away. One of them came hovering back, too delirious to abandon this nectar. He grabbed it from the air. When he opened his fist to make sure, he found it smudged into blood and delicate filaments of leg. The bird he lifted with cupped hands. Once he'd soothed it, he put it back in the box he'd built. Already in it for weight were his coins and the speckled nugget of saxum Mr. Hawkins had given him. He lay a handkerchief across it to screen out the mosquitoes. The bird breathed within, softer than distant crickets.

"You'll have to keep that bird quiet, or I'll kill the damn thing," Dad said next morning as they trudged to the creek. "I slept so bad I'm all out of temper."

"Is that what did it?" Clay said.

Dad turned and backhanded him. He saw the blow coming. He knew he was better off not to try dodging. For just an instant, the side of his face felt hot and wet, but then that sensation sizzled away into mere pain. Clay felt tears come to his eyes. He wouldn't cry, not if he could help it. He hated the smirk he'd get. It occurred to him, for the first time in his life, that he might hit Dad back. He was nowhere near as thick, but almost as tall. The slap hadn't even knocked him down. He might win.

"That's for having a smart mouth," Dad hissed, and stomped on toward the creek. Clay followed. Not that he hadn't daydreamed it many times—hitting his father—but it had never occurred to him as an actual plan. The thought sent fear thrilling through him. Of course, even if he did it, Mama would try to smooth things over. She'd tell him fathers got impatient sometimes, and now was a bad time with all the pressure Dad was under, that he'd sacrificed so much to move them all west for a better life, and so on, and it would end with her telling Clay to apologize.

Now that Dad's back was turned, he wiped at his tears. The corner of his mouth felt wet. His tongue found a little blood there.

Dad stomped into the shallows of the creek, parting the head-high cattails like a curtain. The water rilled in little braids over the rocks beyond. Further still, in a sluggish pool at the far side of the creek, a messy beaver lodge stood. "Look at this!" Dad bellowed. "I don't believe Vinson's done a thing."

He slogged out of the creek, carefully not looking at Clay. Clay could read the bunching muscles of his back. They meant he was halfway between rage and regret. Later there would be an apology, along with an explanation of how Clay had brought it on himself. This time he actually had. Clay took a sort of comfort in that.

"What's that?" Dad said. They'd come near the Great Saxum Rock, which seemed to leer at them from the corners of hollow eyes. Something was bobbing briskly round the bend before it.

It was a dead body, *plain as the dumb look on your face*, Clay wanted to say. Dad would have said exactly that if anybody else had asked. It rolled over in the current, as if turning in its sleep, except that its red eyes—Vinson's eyes—were wide open. Clay felt grateful when the current gently rolled those eyes out of sight again. By then the body had passed them.

"Good God!" Dad said. "Do you think we can catch him?"

"I don't think so," Clay stammered. For once, Dad took his opinion as gospel.

That night the yellow bird screamed loud enough to rattle the panes.

"Quiet!" Clay whispered as he rolled out of bed. "He'll hear you!"

The match he struck showed the bird shivering under fluffed feathers in the box he'd made. A wound had burst open into a red scribble. He put his match to a candle; the wick brought a calmer kind of light. The bird settled under his petting. Still, it was too loud.

"You have to be quiet!" he whispered. He noticed its nostrils, fine as the eyes of needles, where flecks of blood had dried.

The door slammed open. The candle-flame danced. Dad was almost invisible in the buffeting shadows. Clay never saw the blow that decked him. He was suddenly sprawling on the wood floor, aware of his teeth, his skull, like the stones in overripe fruit.

His coins clinked in the box. "Leave my stuff alone!" he said.

"I told you what I'd do," Dad said, with a sort of triumph. Then he was out the door. No use following, and besides, Clay's head tingled. He wasn't sure of his footing.

It was easy to hear Dad's progress. His bare feet on the stairs. Mama's exclamation of "Jonathan!" as he went past their room, as if she could possibly be shocked. The front door opening, crashing back. Clay scrambled to his window and looked down in time to see Dad lumber forth into the moonlight with the box in his hand. The bird shrilled, and kept shrilling until he had carried it far out into the darkness.

Half a dozen skitterfish mouthed at a carcass where it floated, snagged among the cattails. Clay watched with interest. Was it another beaver, maybe? He'd found half a dozen dead and skinned, no doubt the work of Hal Vinson before whatever happened to him. The bits of fur on the carcass suggested beaver, but its skull seemed round enough to be human. For a horrid moment he imagined it as Vinson. Could his body somehow have traveled upstream all this way to lodge beneath the Great Saxum Rock? A skitterfish took hold of the skull with its delicate little hands and turned it gently, as if to afford Clay a better view. He leaned out as far as he dared. The carcass bobbed. The fish fussed with each other for position and kissed its flanks.

A shot rang out. It echoed from the trees behind Clay, then echoed again from the great rock opposite. He nearly lost his balance.

Dad wouldn't put up with poachers. Clay set out to investigate. In a few minutes he'd picked his way across on a beaver dam. He had only a vague sense that the shot had come from near the Rock. He was almost surprised to find confirmation. The doe must have been drinking from the creek in plain sight of him, if only he'd looked. Now she lay quivering. He could smell singed fur from the buckshot wounds.

But where was the hunter? He looked downstream, where cottonwoods crowded in, and upstream, where the dam made the water pool lazy and deep. No human footprint showed on the muddy bank, though the deer's tracks, like double stabs, were clear.

"I shoot from the heavens!" a voice laughed. Clay couldn't, for a long moment, see who had spoken. Then he looked up. Ten feet high, within the hollow cheek of the Rock, leaned Hawkins, brandishing his shotgun. "Animals never think to look up," he added.

"My dad won't like it if he catches you hunting on our land," Clay said. He regretted his words instantly. He sounded stingy as his father.

"I've watched your father at his work," Hawkins smiled. "He never looks up either."

Clay didn't know how to take that. It sounded like a threat.

"Stick with me, kid, and I'll teach you a few things your father never knew."

It was more than a year later when, over supper, they heard a woman scream.

Clay paused with a spoonful of potatoes in hand. The steam of them writhed as it rose.

"Someone needs help," Mama said— exasperated, it seemed, because no one was moving.

"Shows how much you know," Dad smirked. "That's a panther."

"Are you sure?" she said.

"Good God, woman, haven't you heard it these three nights running?" Dad said. "And I've seen its tracks beside the barn. We'll have to hunt it. Liable to take some cattle."

The thought of Dad on a dangerous hunt reminded Clay of his guilty secret, of all the days he'd stolen away from chores to learn tracking and shooting from Hawkins. Now he imagined the panther lurking in the trees, gathering itself for a leap, while his father lumbered heedless beneath.

Serve him right. Yet Clay quivered at the thought.

Along Saxum Creek, the cat tracks ran thick, going both ways. Clay knelt to look at them. Immediately he sensed a creeping danger. Something must be watching him. He rose, held his rifle waist high. He wondered if he could hit a moving target.

As he scanned for movement, he noticed a beaver lodge in the creek. He'd seen this one before; it was among those Dad had made him sketch for Vinson. Its top had ruptured. Some of its sticks lay dragged along the bank. This might be old destruction; it might be Vinson's work.

He waded out to it. A mottled branch along the top seemed to waver like grease on a griddle. He got close enough to breathe on it before he realized its mobile texture meant ants—one file trailing out from undergrowth on the bank, another coming back laden. He wondered what sort of food they were dismantling, crumb by crumb.

He pulled himself up from the water and onto the lodge. It creaked and shifted under his weight. He paused. He was near enough now to see over the rim of the crater. A meaty smell rose from the darkness. He found a match in his shirt pocket and struck it. The flame faltered in the humid air. It made the medley of bones within seem to wriggle. He'd never thought of beavers eating meat. Apparently, on Saxum Creek, they did.

The broken lodge he stumbled on a week later told a clearer story. The tracks of the

panther led down from the shore—the
pugs like a letter M with four little toe-
smudges in front. Two beaver kits
shivered on the inner dome of grass,
nestling on their sides to form a circle.
They would die if he left them. His hands
were reaching in when one of them
barked. It was like oatmeal burbling in a
pot, but shriller. Now that it had sensed
him, it kept up a steady stream of chirps,
asking, he supposed, to be fed. Soon its
sibling joined in.

Dad wouldn't put up with this noise.

Maybe he could hide them in the tool
shed.

Better just to leave them alone. Why
prolong their lives, only to see them killed
later on?

Just then he spotted something
gleaming in the dark. A match showed
him a side-pocket woven of grass, and
within it a handful of saxum nuggets.
Their flecks winked green in the firelight.

The maples shed red leaves and brown
ones. The elms became lacy and beetle-
bitten before they, too, cast off their
clothes. Clay drove their two milch cows

through this rattling litter of leaves one evening, lost in thought. "Too many legs, too smart, too hard to kill"—that was what Hawkins had told them about the animals of Saxum Creek. It seemed to him the beavers had been smart enough to scheme, to somehow kill Vinson when he went to work on their lodges.

And yet the beavers were fewer now. The panther must be taking its toll. It had been a presence on their land for weeks now, calling in the night like a woman with a broken heart, crying until Dad cursed. Its tracks, Hawkins said, showed it to be young, yet big enough to take cattle or kill a man. Many a day, Dad set out with his gun, leaving a list of chores for Clay to finish before sundown.

Something interrupted Clay's thoughts. He took two steps back to be sure what he'd seen. Amid the leaves lay a dead bird. He paused. The cattle knew the way to the barn. The gold shape was battered and dusty, but he recognized it.

There were no ants to trouble its body. They had, he supposed, picked the skeleton the morning after Dad killed the yellow bird. The feathers had not interested them; they remained, an empty suit of clothes for its bones. He was off the usual path by only a yard or so. Maybe the bird had lain here all this time. He poked through the weeds nearby and found the box he'd made, now broken, and even one of the silver dollars it had held.

Of course he had already known what happened to the bird, more or less. Yet the proof hurt him. He felt a headachy pressure behind his eyes, but something in him refused to cry. It was only a bird, after all.

He brought a shovel from the tool shed. As he dug, his own hands, thick like Dad's, somehow made him ashamed.

"Bury him deep," Hawkins smiled, coming up the path with his shotgun. By now Clay was used to his sudden appearances. "Bury him deep; things don't rest easy on Saxum Creek. It's the mineral, you know."

That night the panther shredded his sleep with its calls, and Dad raged through the house. At dawn, Clay opened bleary eyes and decided he'd spend the day trailing it. Both cows were restless while he squeezed their tender udders. "You heard it, too?" he asked.

On his way to the creek, the rifle propped on his shoulder, he was startled to a stop by the sight of Dad's eyes. They looked at him imploringly. He could hardly understand what he was seeing. The eyes were low and upside down. It took a long moment for him to see, among the light-brown maple leaves, the identically colored shape of the panther. It lay draped on Dad, partly obscuring his form, and held him in its paws. It glared jealously at Clay. Its eyes were red and familiar. After a moment it seemed to decide he was no threat. It licked Dad on the face, the neck. Until Dad shuddered, Clay had thought him dead. Certainly he was bloody, though the red leaves among the brown ones made that hard to sort out.

"Go home and bolt the door, Son," Dad said with surprising calm. "If you miss from this distance, he might charge you." The panther growled softly, as if offended by the remark.

Clay brought his rifle to his shoulder. His sights lined up—not on the panther's face, but on his father's.

The possibilities dizzied him. People would think it was an accident.

If only Dad hadn't just now said something kind, something to keep him safe.

Yet killing him might be a kindness in itself. Surely his wounds were fatal?

These thoughts transpired like a syrupy dream. He was aware, at the same time, that he'd taken only a second, that he should take even a little longer with his shot. He should sight carefully; then still his breath, as Hawkins had taught him; then squeeze, rather than pull. He would not get another shot. The panther would melt away into the undergrowth, or else charge and end his troubles.

It glanced up with its rheumy red eyes. He sighted between them. Despite everything. The fur was lighter there, almost white, but peppered with fine black hairs. He stilled his breath. The panther turned its full resentful gaze on Clay, but he was already squeezing the trigger.

The shot flipped it end over end. It landed on its feet and dashed to the left, knocking leaves into the air. It crouched, lashed its tail. The tail straightened. Clay wondered whether he should pelt it with rocks to make sure it was dead.

"That was a good shot, son," Dad coughed. Blood bubbled out of his mouth.

He was too big to carry. In the end, Clay brought him home in the wheelbarrow. "Damnedest thing," he said. "What did I ever do to get Vinson mad at me?"

It reeked of lunacy. A dying man's hallucinations. It wasn't Vinson who had hurt him. Yet it was! The eyes had looked right, anyway.

"You sent him out to kill the beavers, and they killed him."

"I figure it's the creek. A cub drinks where that mineral mixes in, and a dead body besides. It grows up wrong."

"Stay still," Clay said, and paused to lift the barrow over a fallen elm branch. "Every time you talk, more blood pumps out." His back crackled under the strain, but the barrow came over, and Dad didn't fall out or even criticize. He only huffed with pain as the barrow hit the ground again.

"You'll have to go back for our rifles, son," Dad said. "I hate for you to risk it, but those cost money."

Going back was the worst part, worse than Mama's crying, worse than the ragged new orifice they found when they cut Dad's shirt away. Clay, unarmed now, expected the panther behind every bush. He paused for a long time to study a forked elm. The shape within it might be a feline face glaring at him. When he finally dared another step, the shape resolved into nothing, into the grain of the bark.

At the bend of the path where he'd shot it, he was surprised to see the panther lying on the bare patch exactly as he'd left it. He noticed now that it had two tails—the one that had lashed so furiously in its death throes, and another curled around a hind leg.

In a dream, Clay found himself small again. Navigating across the kitchen floor in the dark, he passed beneath the table without ducking. Something outside was asking quiet, liquid questions, and he meant to find it. Out on the starlit porch he noticed nothing out of the ordinary, until the noise came again. It was coming from Dad's ladder-back chair. He hadn't seen the owl that sat there like a man, camouflaged in feathers the color of pine bark. He gasped to see what it was doing: caressing live coals, making the feathered hands singe and stink. It looked at Clay with eyes the size of silver dollars. Their irises, however, were not silver, but striations of pale maple, amber, doe's hide. He concluded they'd once been black but were, from gazing at songbirds with predatory intent, rapidly growing lighter and brighter.

"Was that you, talking?" Clay said. His voice rang childish in his own ears.

The owl blinked, thank God; its stare was about to make Clay run.

"Have you seen the finches on the fence?" Clay said, and turned to point. Something cold pinched his spine, the same trick Dad used to play on him when he was little.

"Did you do that?" he said, trying to placate the thing, looking for somewhere to run. This time the owl didn't even blink. By now the black middles of its eyes floated like bullets in molten gold.

As he woke, his fear drained away faster than he could grasp it, leaving a sadness he had rarely known. He thought of the yellow bird, singing helplessly in its box. He'd held it in his overalls next to his heart, had found its blood in the patterns of his palms, had kept it with his treasures, even after its droppings soiled the box. He tried to remember the beauty of its song, but really it had never sung beautifully, not that he had heard. Its every sound was a shriek of pain or the mournful cooing of pain briefly eased. And then its body had turned up just before Dad got hurt, mingling recriminations with his worry.

'That was a good shot, son,' his father had said. 'My boy's good at drawing.'

Downstairs, he found his parents before the fire. On the settee, Mama twitched in a bad dream of her own. Dad sat in the stuffed chair where they'd propped him to keep him from choking on his own blood. The toe of his left boot, the one he hadn't let them remove because of the pain, smoked. Clay knelt before him to shift his leg. It was heavy and cold. Clay looked up into a face flaccid, critical of nothing. The boot let loose one last wisp. Dad must have stretched it too close to the fire in his death-throes.

I'll bury him deep, Clay thought, already knowing he'd see the man with molten eyes again in dreams. Things don't rest easy on Saxum Creek.

See Gordon Grice's story "If Gold Runs Red"
online at Metaphorosis.
If you liked it, leave a comment. Authors love
that!
Remember to subscribe to our e-mail updates so
you'll know when new stories are posted.

About the story

Somewhere I picked up a warped, water-stained, moldy volume of Chinese folklore called *The Man Who Sold a Ghost*, translated into English by Yan Hsien-Yi and Gladys Yang. It was packed with gruesome tales of were-foxes and greedy specters. I liked the poetic flavor of one from around 500 AD. It's about a boy rescuing an injured bird. The bird turns out to be a god. He helps the boy get good jobs and such. Actually, I only liked the beginning. The divine explanation and the job-advancement didn't do much for me. I decided to warp the premise to suit my own tastes. Early on, I changed the setting to the rural Western landscape I knew. In later drafts, the boy took on a troubled family life, while the landscape got polluted by a meteoric rock with uncanny effects on living things—a science fiction premise to replace the god I'd sent packing. What I enjoyed most was figuring out the effects the meteorite might have on different animals, from birds to beavers. Really, I had too much fun with that; I ended up cutting unnecessary scenes about earthworms, beetles, owls, and finches. I took the scene of a dead man rolling down a river from a real murder case I covered as a reporter. A witness's bizarre description had stuck with me for years, waiting for a suitable story to fit into.

A question for the author

Q: What made you start writing?

A: I got the urge to write as soon as I learned to read, but I was in college before I wrote a story I liked. My attempts before that ended with frustration, pencil-smears, opening lines too dumb to write past. What broke me through was discovering Edgar Allan Poe's "The Facts in the Case of M. Valdemar." The story started in clinical detachment and ended in one of the most disturbing gore scenes I'd ever read—exactly the sort of scene my teachers had told me to quit writing. It wasn't the gore itself that impressed me. It was how much Poe made it mean, how powerful it felt, how seamlessly he led me through reasonable-seeming steps to a monstrous conclusion. He became my model.

About the author

Gordon Grice is freelance magazine writer and wandering college lecturer whose literary course topics have included horror, homicide, science fiction, monsters, Edgar Allan Poe, and man-eating animals. He frequently teaches creative writing for the UCLA Extension Writer's Program. He and his wife have three sons and two pet tarantulas.

GordonGrice.com, @GordonGrice

.

Bas Relief

Joshua Grasso

Sveta twisted and turned in the mirror, lifting her shirt to inspect her stomach, flattering herself that it looked harder, firmer, than it had last week. But no, she could easily pinch the flesh into an unsightly fat roll as usual. She pulled up her sleeves, inspecting every inch of her arm, hoping against hope to find something rough and scaly. Again, nothing but soft, pale skin, or what the upperclassmen liked to call 'soft serve'. All quivering adolescent flesh and nothing substantial.

The only thing remotely tough on her body was the crusty elbow scab she had scraped with a key out of boredom. There were people she knew—well, they weren't friends, of course—who could file down keys and fingernails against their skin. Even one guy whose head was so rock-hard that you could break a board over it. She had watched him once during third-period gym, and he just laughed, saying he didn't feel a thing and asking his pals to do it again and again.

Out of sheer desperation, she peeled off her socks and inspected her toes and heels, hoping the skin had hardened, dried out. But even they were baby-smooth and without blemish. There were a few girls who couldn't even wear shoes anymore, as their toes were granite-hard and could deflate soccer balls with a single kick. But after all, only those who didn't change played sports after high school, since flexibility was the surest obstacle to upward mobility.

She must have been ignoring her texts, because when her phone rang, she saw Malorie's name flash over the screen—and she never called.

"Bitch, do you ever look at your phone?" Malorie said, with a laugh.

"Sorry, I'm getting ready—running late. I'll see you in a few."

"Not today you won't. I'm sick off my ass. I might miss the entire week, who knows?"

"Maly, not again!" Sveta said, throwing herself on the bed. "You can't keep doing this. You've already missed, what, ten or twelve days? You'll get suspended."

"Whatever. We don't belong there anyway, among those privileged, petrified snobs. I'm sick of pretending I give a shit. What's the point of even graduating at this point?"

"Because otherwise you'll spend the rest of your life delivering take-out in this two-bit town. Come on, it's just a few more months. Get your ass in the car."

"Sorry, I really am coughing my brains out. *Cough, cough.* See, you can't fake that."

"Bullshit."

"Just take the bus and stop bitching. Or go pass the driving exam already. I mean, a lot of people fail it twice."

"I've already missed the bus, and if you don't take me...I have to ask her. Please don't make me ask her!"

"You two need some quality time together; you'll thank me later. Say hi to the clones in Calc!"

She wasted five minutes trying to call Malorie back, but she never answered. That only left her enough time to catch her mother before she left for work and ask her—or in this case, beg her—to take Sveta to school, which would add twenty minutes to her commute. The second she walked downstairs and they locked eyes her mother knew. She only shook her head and muttered, "Three minutes, and I'm leaving with or without you."

The drive to school was more strained than usual. Sveta sat in the passenger seat, clutching her backpack against her chest, watching the traffic lights zoom past. Her mother's eyes kept cutting over to her, as if trying to pry through the clothes and see some tell-tale sign of transformation. Even as a child, her mother's hands would sweep over her flesh, poking here, prodding there, looking for resistance. *There's still time, you're still young,* she always told her, but it never sounded encouraging.

"You know, maybe you should see someone? Like a therapist? They say it's often a mental block, and you used to have those nightmares, remember?"

Used to. Still did. Always did. But it was better for her mother not to know what kept her awake at night.

"Maybe it's just not my time yet, okay?" Sveta replied. "You're a late bloomer. And Malorie, she still isn't showing."

"Knowing her parents, I'm not surprised," her mother said, with a snicker. "But you come from a long line of *rockers*. Okay, it started late for me—and like a lot of women, just one arm—but look at your grandparents: they were planted on the hill in their forties. It's inspiring to see them looking down on us, along with the rest of our family...so many generations of Beckers and Burlatskys."

She interrupted her speech to honk at someone who had cut her off, then continued.

"I'm just saying, you're almost eighteen...some kids are already thinking about where they'll be planted. If you already had a stiff arm or leg, we could reserve a spot somewhere on the hill, maybe just behind the house next to Daddy? You want to settle down before all the good places are taken."

"I mean, I guess...I just wish everyone didn't make such a big deal about it. It'll happen eventually, won't it?"

"For most people, yes, but you have to be a little proactive," she said, thoughtfully. "Not to speak ill of your friend, but Malorie lives in a trailer park. Her parents never settled down, and I doubt she will, either. Can you imagine, spending your entire life running around, never knowing your place? I knew early on where I wanted to be, who I was going to marry, even before this," she said, raising her arm. "And your father—"

"Can we not?" Sveta said, burying her face in her bag.

Her father, the famous *rock star* himself, who was in a wheelchair at eighteen. He had even made the local paper; a miracle of science, they called him. By the time she was six he was immobilized in the bedroom, just a living rock that would greet her and kiss her goodnight. A few years later they moved him to the yard, since the doctors said he was still *there*, still with them, though they couldn't say for how long. It only took a year before they felt it was time, and moved him up with his parents on the hill, another Becker to watch over the generations-yet-unborn.

"Sveta, you should be proud of him. I know it's tough not to have him around, but he did this for the family...he wanted the best for all of us."

Honestly, she barely remembered him as a living, functional parent. He had always been that *thing* in the bedroom, and she used to dread going in there at all, which was mostly reserved for bedtimes and birthdays. She hated that look in his eyes, which always seemed distant, like he didn't even know who she was. There were statues that looked kinder, more alive.

"Does it hurt?" she asked, after a pause.

"Does what? This?" her mother asked, holding up her 'good' arm, the one that was cracked and gray. "No, not at all. It's just heavier, that's all. If anything, it gives me comfort. I feel like I've become whole, like nothing can hurt me."

"Really? But what happens when you can't move? When you just have to sit around all day, having people wait on you? Doesn't that scare you?"

"If I didn't have such a loving daughter in my life, yes, it might," her mother said, with a smile. "But I know you'll take care of me. And then I'll watch over you, along with your father, from the top of the hill. You can bring your own kids up to see me, and they can hug me, climb me, whatever they like. We'll still be one big happy family."

"I guess so," Sveta said, seeing her school swing into view through the window.

"So listen, I made an appointment for you next week...the therapist came highly recommended," her mother said. "Just try it, just for a session or two. It might help. Because there's no reason you can't do it...there's nothing wrong with you. Really."

She said that last *really* as if convincing herself, lest she see her daughter as a failed experiment, someone unworthy of the Becker-Burlatsky line. She gave Sveta an affectionate pat on the shoulder as she pulled into the lot and wished her a good day. Sveta gave a miserable smile and ducked out of the car, feeling that she had survived this conversation mostly intact (unlike last time, when they had stopped talking to each other for a week).

Still, the pressure to conform and change seemed more intense than usual; not just from her mother, but from Malorie, too. It had become their only topic of conversation, and the closer they got to graduation, the more she felt she had made a decision, even without making one. It made her examine everyone with new eyes today, seeing those who *were* and those who *weren't*. All the jocks seemed to lumber about, some dragging stone legs across the floor or with faces almost set, so that you couldn't tell if they were happy or pissed off. Most of the popular kids—probably for this very reason—seemed to be well advanced, a few using crutches to get about, but one with a neck so stiff he had to turn his body simply to look at his friends. There were only a handful of girls like her who seemed normal, who moved around efficiently but seemed to hide in the background, with no infirmities to boast of. Had it always been like this? Or were people changing faster, younger, so they could be as safe and watchful as their parents?

At lunch, instead of sampling the cafeteria fare, she ducked into the library and pulled up the yearbook archive on the school's website. She scrolled through the decades, going as far back as the 1950's, watching long hair and t-shirts gradually fade into sideburns and neckties, until finally everyone became indistinguishable from the teachers: frame after frame of well-coiffed girls with giant glasses, and crew-cut boys with funeral-director suits. At first it seemed depressing, as if every one of those 1950's kids was half-chiseled out of marble.

Yet at second glance she wasn't so sure. The further back she went, the more the students seemed to have eyes. Naturally, they all *had eyes*, but these seemed alive, full of mystery and excitement. As she went forward, the stares seemed to dim, to look away, to die out. In recent years, she could sense a kind of dullness creep in, a sense that the kids had nothing to live for. Almost like the transformation had started from the inside-out.

Was that how she felt, watching everyone else turn to stone like clockwork? Was that why she still had nightmares, why she was secretly terrified of seeing a patch of gray or a finger locked in place? Of course she knew it was a good thing; she had seen all the movies and read all the books, all those glorious couples turning to stone together as the sun set behind them. Her mother called it *going back to the earth*, and said there was nothing more natural, more romantic.

How strange that people used to die in wrinkled, useless skin that had to be buried out of sight and forgotten. Why settle for tombstones when you could become a living monument for those you loved?

And yet it terrified her. She still woke up most nights in a cold sweat from dreams where she was mounted like a *bas relief* over the fireplace. Her parents and friends would gather to inspect her, offering toasts, saying how wonderfully she completed the room. No matter how hard she screamed they only shook their heads, assuring her that the feeling would pass as soon as she let it go. And then she saw all the other terrified faces on the wall, all of them frozen in screaming stone.

She became so lost in these thoughts that she missed both bells and was late to Biology. By the time she arrived, students were already working in pairs on their next experiment. Her normal partner wasn't there, so she had to sit awkwardly at her desk, waiting for the teacher to notice. She thought about asking to be a third wheel in someone else's group, but she could see the looks on their faces; she was on her own. Mr. Malkin, largely immobile behind his desk, suddenly noticed her and waved imperiously.

"Miss Becker, don't just sit there. Your partner's out sick. You can pick up the lab when he returns. Here, take this to Study Hall," he said, handing her a pass.

"Study Hall? But Mr. Malkin, I can't go there! I mean, I'm not...can't I just work with someone here?" she asked, panicked.

"If you had come earlier, maybe, but I can't stop everyone just for you. Now here, take the pass. I have a lab to conduct."

"Mr. Malkin, please, you don't understand—"

"You've only got yourself to blame," he said, with a look that suggested he wasn't just talking about class.

Horrified, she took the pass and felt the whispers of mockery behind her. Study Hall was reserved for students who were on the fast-track to immobility. It allowed them a chance to take all their normal classes in a single room, since they couldn't possibly make it across the building, much less to lunch, between bells. If she walked in there like this, on both feet, without crutches or an obvious impairment, the jokes would never end. She almost thought about ditching school entirely, but without a ride she wouldn't get far. The only other choice was to hide in the bathroom until the bell rang, but that's where the druggies hung out, and she wasn't stoned enough for them, either.

She opened the door to Study Hall and the students—a small group of twelve or so—looked up from their desks, students she knew from junior high and grade school. She had watched them grow up, sometimes being friends with them, sometimes not, until they all got lost in a blur of adolescence. Surprisingly, no one laughed or objected to her presence. The teacher gestured for her pass and then went back to his book, similarly indifferent. Sveta scanned the room, trying to think which student she would piss off the least by sitting beside them.

Helen Canevaro. They had been friends for a short space in third or fourth grade, but something had happened, a spat at a birthday party, she didn't remember. She still fondly remembered spending the night at Helen's house once, reading manga and watching old horror movies until three in the morning. Helen looked up at her with a smile and said hello. Gratefully, Sveta slung her backpack over the chair and sat down, smiling back.

"Hey, good to see you," Sveta said, quietly. "Sorry, I know I don't belong here, I'm kind of a loser, but I got kicked out of class. No lab partner."

"No, it's cool, I've only been here for a few weeks," Helen said, gesturing to her foot. "I don't feel like I belong here, either."

Sveta looked down at her right foot, which at first resembled a mud-stained cast. Upon closer inspection, she could see what used to be toes encrusted with a jumble of mottled stone. Otherwise, though, Helen looked completely normal, her bare arms untouched, except for a small bird tattoo near her left elbow. Their eyes met, and Sveta was startled how much Helen looked like that one girl from the crazy Swedish movie where they sacrificed people. Maybe that was the real reason they'd stopped hanging out all those years ago. Sometimes girls could tell when she looked at them a certain way, or for too long, and didn't like it.

"Is it hard...you know, getting around?" Sveta asked.

"Yeah, it's kind of a drag," she said, nodding. "It goes all the way up to my knee. I woke up one morning and it was like that, no warning. My parents were thrilled. They would have bought me a car if they thought I could drive it."

"Shit," Sveta said, with a laugh. "I don't know whether to say *congratulations* or *I'm sorry*."

"Both, I guess. What about you? Any signs yet?"

"No, nothing. I'm a total failure. The disappointment of my entire clan," she said dramatically.

"I doubt that. You were someone people always looked up to. I remember when... well, never mind, it's silly."

"No, what?" Sveta asked. "Come on, tell me."

"Oh, you probably won't remember... but back in third grade, we went to the county fair together. Your mom took us."

"Oh right, of course," Sveta said, starting to remember.

"Anyway, there was that booth where you had to throw baseballs at bottles. I sucked, couldn't hit even one. But you hit every one, over and over again. There was a crowd of people watching you, cheering you on, and you kept going until the guy kicked you out. Said you were cheating."

"Oh yeah, I forgot all about that! What a dick."

"But you still won that giant rabbit: it was ridiculously big, cotton-candy pink, with these huge floppy ears, remember? And you gave it to me, even though it was yours, even though I begged you to keep it. You even told me—I know, it sounds silly now—that I was your inspiration."

Sveta didn't have a clear vision of winning the rabbit or giving it to Helen, though the general impression rang true. She only remembered a vague, warm sensation in her gut whenever she thought about their brief friendship. It was still one of the happiest times of her life.

"Sorry I made you keep it. Hopefully you got rid of it in the morning."

"No way, I still have her!" Helen said, eyes wide. "She sits right on my bed... sometimes I even use her as a pillow."

"*Her?* Don't tell me you named it?" Sveta said.

"Of course: Anastasia! I think your name inspired me. Whenever I see her, I always remember you, that night we spent together. I hated that we stopped being friends."

"Yeah, I wonder why we did? I guess it doesn't matter anymore, we were just kids. Maybe we can...you know, start over? Especially since we're stuck here together."

"But only here until your lab partner comes back to class, right? Are they really sick?" Helen asked, cautiously.

"I don't know, maybe. I barely even know the guy," she said, with a shrug.

"Good...I don't like competition," Helen replied.

It was only after the bell rang and they went their separate ways that Sveta realized she still had a crush on Helen, and her third-grade game had been smoother than she thought.

As it happened, her lab partner, Sam Dickey, was having unexpected complications from his sudden change. It happened sometimes. They didn't like to talk about it, but a few students were hospitalized when the change was too abrupt, or when it started in the wrong place. She knew at least one kid had died when his heart turned to stone. That was what scared her the most, the Russian roulette of the transformation. It was almost like someone was having a sick joke at their expense, one time choosing something ridiculous, like an ear, and another, an essential organ. She suddenly felt guilty that she didn't even remember what Sam looked like, other than his glasses, which were always slipping off.

However, after a few days of Study Hall, she fell into a comfortable routine with Helen, no longer worried about being witty or stupid or whatever. Mostly she just spent time observing Helen, noticing all the little things hidden in plain view, but which took days and weeks to pick up. Case in point, she realized Helen was filling up page after page with elaborate arabesques, which sometimes coalesced into familiar shapes and faces. Once, without trying to be too sneaky about it, she spied a dreamy portrait emerge on the margins of Helen's homework.

"Damn, did you do that just on the spot?" she asked.

"Oh—yeah, I mean, I'm just scribbling. It helps me think, it always has. It's nothing really."

"If you do that, you must have other stuff, too, like where you're really trying. Can you show me?"

Helen grew a bit red at the suggestion, though it was clear that the scribbles were a subtle invitation to see more. But now she was nervous to go all the way.

"Well, look, don't read too much into this...but I wanted to give you this. I was just worried you would think, *wow, that's weird* or something. But I made it for you."

Helen unzipped her backpack and removed a sketch pad smudged with charcoal on the cover. She opened the cover and flipped past several pages of abstract images, still lives, landscapes, houses. Then she came to one of the last pages, which, after a grin, she nudged over toward Sveta. Sveta could tell what it was even upside-down, even before her eyes really put it together.

It was a portrait of her, a bit idealized, of course, but taken by someone who had paid attention, who caught more than just the shoulder-length hair, the freckles, the little gap in her teeth. She saw her hesitation, her excitement, her awkwardness, her beauty. That was Sveta's first thought when she really took in the portrait: *Jesus, she's gorgeous.* Because she really felt like she was looking at Helen looking at her, and so much of Helen had bled through that it made the portrait feel like a warm embrace that wouldn't let go.

"My God, Helen...this is wonderful. I mean, I wish I looked like that. When did you do this?"

"A few nights ago. I got bored doing my homework...or rather, I couldn't concentrate on my homework. I kept thinking about you."

So there, I said it, her eyes seemed to announce. They were wide-awake eyes, right there, looking to the future. Like those fifties kids in the yearbook, but no longer carved in stone.

"It's wonderful, I love it," Sveta said, stroking it with her hand. "It's perfect."

"Then it was worth doing," Helen said, with a smile. "It's yours, of course. I still have the original."

"Where, in your head?"

Helen gave a little nod that suggested both yes and no. They didn't say another word for the rest of class, allowing Sveta to replay the scene over and over until she knew it by heart.

Sveta waited for Helen after school, saw her coming out of the building on her crutches, her dead leg holding her back, bringing tears of frustration. When she suddenly looked up and saw Sveta, her face went blank, the pain retreating. Then her eyes lit up again. Sveta didn't look at who was watching, what they might think (or what she might think tomorrow). She went right up to Helen and said something, she didn't even remember what, and kissed her. Really quickly, before either of them could think twice. Helen's eyes stayed wide-open in surprise, only closing as she pulled away, drinking it in.

"That's for the drawing," Sveta said, awkwardly.

"I have a few more, if you want to see them. But I keep them at home."

"I want to see everything. I mean, if you'll let me...if I'm not being, you know, too weird or something."

"Whatever...I like weird girls."

A car pulled up just behind them, which Sveta recognized from the general cacophony (shuddering engine, muffled sounds of Black Sabbath) as Malorie's car. She tried to ignore it and steal as much time as she could, but Malorie laid on the horn: a long, impatient blast. Sveta gave a backwards wave in Malorie's direction.

"Shit, I gotta go. My ride. You want to come? We can take you—"

"No, my mom insists on picking me up. But thanks. I'll text you later, okay?"

Another honk. Sveta gave Helen a quick squeeze of the hand and darted into the passenger seat of the 'Gremlin' as they called it, though she had no idea what brand or model it was. Malorie zoomed off and even went between the parked buses with their STOP signs extended. A few kids flipped her off.

"I'd be doing them a favor," she muttered. "So what, are you hanging out with her now?"

"Yeah, I mean, we're friends," Sveta said, cautiously. "I met her in Study Hall. She's funny, you'd like her."

"I heard she was a stuck-up bitch. But, I mean, if *you* like her."

"I do. She's cool. So, you actually came to school today. What's the occasion?"

"Girl, I guess I'm celebrating," she said, accelerating dramatically out of the parking lot. "I tried to text you, but you were too busy with what's-her-face."

"Celebrating? Why, did Steve send you a dick-pic or something?"

"Honestly, they look the same as his selfies, so who knows? But for real, check this shit out," she said, revealing her left hand, which she had kept hidden at her side.

Flashing it in Sveta's face, she revealed four fingers that were completely stone, with only one, the pinky, unscathed. Sveta shrieked and immediately grabbed it, running her fingers over each one, amazed and terrified by the transformation. Only a few days ago Malorie had made fun of all the *stoners*, as she jokingly called them, comparing the stratification of torsos and biceps. But now she seemed almost giddy over her change, having already posted it across social media, where, she explained, it already had hundreds of likes.

"My parents are flipping out," Malorie said, trying unsuccessfully to wiggle her fingers. "You know how they said I was on my own for college? Well, guess who just put up five thousand bucks?"

"You're joking! Really? Just because of this?"

"Hell yeah, because of this. A lot of people say if you get fingers first, that's a good sign. It means you're as good as gold by your twenties. So if I can get into State, or even one of the liberal arts schools, I might jumpstart fingers into an arm and a leg—or hell, even a torso!"

"But weren't you going to take a gap year or something? So you could travel the country, hike all over the Southwest? Remember the postcard I sent you of the giant saguaro? You were even going to get a tattoo."

Malorie frowned at the reminder, clearly from a different time, a different life. The world before she knew she had a future, or a body worth investing in.

"I mean...that would be cool, but I can't just waste an entire year when I could, you know, be getting ahead. And why go to Arizona or wherever when there are so many good colleges here?"

"And that's what you really want?" Sveta said, hesitantly. "You just seemed so happy, like you had everything figured out. This shouldn't change things completely."

"But it does, like a million percent! I never thought I would have a chance to settle down, find a place on the hill where everyone can see me. And who knows, after college I might be solid rock. Think what that would mean to my parents!"

"To be a statue before you're thirty?" she said, unable to hide her disappointment. "You saw what happened to my father; I barely knew him, Maly. What if you have kids? Is that how you want them to remember you? Because they won't remember you at all. You'll just be that thing in the garden, or up on the hill, reminding them to study hard and eat their vegetables."

Malorie abruptly switched lanes and pulled into an abandoned gas station where they used to hang out, where Malorie allegedly made out with some guy who just graduated. The car slammed to a halt and Malorie just glared at her, her soft hand gripping the wheel.

"I thought you would be happy for me," she said, her deep voice cracking. "You're the only person I really wanted to tell, Sveta. Because I knew you would give a shit. Or at least understand. I wasn't supposed to change and you know it. My parents are soft-skinned, trailer-trash rednecks. And I'm trailer-trash, too."

"No, Maly, I do—I get it. I *am* happy for you. I just don't think you should be in such a hurry to be like everyone else. You're different than them, you always said so. That's why we're friends. And we'll still be friends, no matter what."

"What the fuck do you know about me?" Malorie said, giving her a shove. "Maybe I've wanted this my whole life but was too scared to ask? Maybe I didn't want to be disappointed like I always am? People don't give two shits about me around here, Sveta. I don't have parents, a reputation like yours. I'll always be *that girl* to them."

"Who cares? I like *that girl*, don't you? And since when do you need them to like you? It's us against the world, remember?"

Malorie gave a world-weary laugh, as if she had heard this before, many times, in fact, and still didn't buy it. Sveta tried to backtrack, but Malorie cut her off, rolling down the window and yelling "bullshit!" at the top of her lungs. Sveta waited for the moment to pass, for Malorie to realize she was overacting and apologize, but it seemed she was just warming up.

"We were never on the same side," Malorie said, eyes flashing. "You're still the same old Sveta, slumming it with me until you find something better. But you don't know the first thing about me...like the reason I hate your guts."

"Do tell," Sveta muttered.

"You're everything I want to be, everything I tried to believe in. You made me feel that it was okay to be who I was. But then I started to see that you didn't even believe in yourself. People used to look up to you, you know? You were the girl *most likely to succeed* and shit. But now...they talk a lot of shit behind your back. They think you've given up; we all do."

"Why, because I'm not practicing to become a lawn ornament? Is that what little kids really dream of doing when they grow up? Why can't we look around, get lost, not try to be exactly like our parents? Why is everyone in such a rush to do nothing for the rest of their lives?"

"Actually, I'm trying *not* to be like my parents," Malorie said, sucking her teeth. "But I'd like to see how far you get with what's-her-name. You think she really cares about you? Today, maybe, but tomorrow she's going to want something real, something lasting. I know I do."

"Then lucky for me she's not like you," Sveta snapped. "No, she's the person I thought you were, the one I felt safe with, who I trusted more than anyone on earth. But I guess friendship's only skin deep... so you'll need a new friend to go with your fucked-up hand."

They drove home in silence, and when they pulled up to Sveta's house, Malorie just sat there, idling. Sveta just sat there, too, trying to think of whether to salvage their relationship or blow it to hell. Malorie beat her to it.

"I love how no one's supposed to change but you," she said, looking away. "I have to remain the fuck-up, the loser, while you figure it out. And once you do, you sure as hell won't wait for me. You'll leave me in the dust."

"Maly, that's not true. I've always had your back."

"You mean you've *held me* back. When I talked about college, or having kids, or anything you don't agree with, it's always *don't do it, it's not you, you'll regret it*. But what if I don't have the same regrets as you?"

"So your answer is to do what everyone else does, to follow them off the same fucking cliff? That's your idea of finding yourself? No, you're smarter than that."

"Everyone goes there for a reason," Malorie said, coldly. "It's what we all secretly want. Like falling in love, having a family. No one stays in the valley unless they have to, even if they lie to themselves and say they prefer it. Life looks better up on the hill, and you know it. At least, your father did."

"Fuck off, Malorie," she said, and opened the door.

"You first," Malorie returned.

As soon as Sveta got out, Malorie sped away, music blasting. Sveta knew she wouldn't see her again for months, maybe not ever. Now she had no one to talk to,

no one to console her for being different,
no one to confide in about her feelings for
Helen. Of course, that's what choosing
your own path was all about: being alone,
choosing the road less traveled by. She
had to have faith in the destination, in
ending up far away in some happily-ever-
after, even if it never was. All the same,
the conversation hit its mark, and she
replayed Malorie's words and her
responses far more than she cared to.
Even when Helen started texting her after
dinner, she was only half-listening,
thinking about *who* Helen was talking to:
the now-her or the one-to-come? The one
who had rock legs like Helen did, or the
loser who never would?

After a few days, Sveta had made her
decision: she and Helen had to break up.
Partly it was everything Malorie had told
her; partly it was her own fear of
commitment. But what really clinched it
was the meme making the rounds of the
school, a picture of two people playing
Paper-Scissors-Rock, the hands of one
opponent forming scissors, the other
forming rock. On the 'rock' someone had
Photoshopped a picture of Helen's head,
and on the 'scissors', Sveta's. Though the
words of the meme had a few variations,

the most consistent one said *Happy Valentine's Day*, with a copy even making its way to her locker at school. The message was clear: rock always beats scissors, and not even love can change the rules of the game. She shuddered to think how often Helen had seen it, and what she must have thought the first, second, and fiftieth time it swam through her feed.

Sveta had to tell her face-to-face, and it had to be at school, so she wouldn't waver and change her mind at the last minute. Of course, it was harder now that Sveta's bio partner had returned and she was back in class doing make-up. Worse still, without Malorie, her mother had to pick her up from school, and she was always there at 3:15 on the dot. So Sveta had about five minutes to waylay Helen, find somewhere semi-private, and tell her the truth. She spent the entire day planning her route, worried about the distance between their rooms and the congestion in the hallway. When the release bell finally rang, she was the first one out the door, pushing and prodding her way across the building to Study Hall, which was precariously close to the exit. A few minutes late, and Helen would slip through the doors and make it into her mom's car before Sveta could say a word.

She made it in record time, just as people were starting to trickle out of other rooms, though Study Hall seemed comfortably full (it took them much longer to leave, obviously). Sveta flattened herself against the wall, eyes picking out every jock and bonehead who left the room, excited—yet crushed—when it wasn't Helen. Seven or eight people came out, then a few more, then one more...then the teacher himself, who flicked off the lights.

Holy shit, where was she?

She knew Helen was here today, because she had said she had a Calc test and couldn't chat over breakfast. Frantic, Sveta began sweeping up and down the hallways, looking for any sign of her presence. She checked both of their lockers (nope), circled back to her last-hour class (no one), and even checked the bathrooms, trying to match the shoes beneath each of the stalls (Nikes; Helen only wore Converse). After five or six minutes she knew it was too late, that somehow she had missed Helen, even though she had covered all the bases and left nothing to chance.

As her heart stopped racing, she became aware of a steady, pulsating hum just around or behind her. Shit, her phone! In her anxiety she had missed an entire stream of texts from Helen. Pulling them up, they all basically said, *Where are you? Really need to talk! Meet me in the locker room. Are you coming? Sveta? Hello???*

It took her another three or four minutes to make her way to the locker room (the hallways were packed now), but it was a well-chosen spot, completely dead. She found Helen sitting in a dark corner of the room on a bench, hugging her knees while she stared down at her phone, waiting for a reply. Sveta swept in and started apologizing, saying she was sorry but they really had to talk, it wouldn't take a minute...but that's as far as she got.

Even as she was explaining, her mind was processing Helen's face and expression. She had been crying. Her eyes were red and there were tissues all over the floor, so she had obviously been here awhile. She must have skipped out early to come here, which explained why Sveta hadn't seen her in Study Hall. But wait, had Helen figured it out? No way, she had been way too careful—and hell, she hadn't even known it herself until just this morning. Sveta walked over and took her hand, squeezing it.

"My God, Helen. What happened?"

Helen gave a little laugh, her expression more happy-sad than distraught, her eyes burning with some hidden passion she couldn't betray. Helen stood up and pulled her close. They embraced, and Helen whispered something in her ear, which sounded like, *Well, I guess I'm all yours now*. What did that mean? As they embraced, Sveta instinctively reached out to support her, since without her crutches there's no way Helen wouldn't—

"Holy shit, your crutches! Helen, where...?"

She was standing straight on both legs, her eyes brimming with tears.

"Sveta, it's gone. Just like that. I woke up this morning...and it was gone. I was too scared to tell you. I made up the Calc test. I've been working towards it all day."

Open-mouthed, Sveta looked down at Helen's bare feet (she had taken off both shoes and socks) and saw two beautiful feet, painted nails and all. She didn't know what to say or think, so she sputtered with a kind of choking laugh, which made Helen laugh even harder.

"I wanted so badly for it to go away. Every night I begged God or whoever was listening to get rid of it. I didn't want anything to take me away from you. And now...well, I don't know what to think. But I'm happy...I *think*!"

"I don't understand, it's gone, like, really gone?" Sveta said, shaking her head. "So you're not...you're not going to be one of them? You can do that?"

"I mean, it's happened before, you hear stories, but I didn't believe them. I guess it helps if you're really in love," she said, looking up at her. "Sorry if that freaks you out, but that's where we are right now. I'm in love with you, and I want you to know that I gave this up, all of it, for you."

Sveta started crying, and she just stood there, pressing her head against Helen's, feeling happier than she knew what to do with. Sveta realized how stupid she had been to come here, to say what she thought was kindness. It would have been kinder to simply tell her the truth: that she was scared. Scared to fall in love, scared that Helen had made a mistake, scared that she would have to watch Helen figure it out in slow motion.

"But what about your parents? They were so happy...what are you going to tell them?" Sveta asked.

"I don't know; I don't care. They'll just have to deal with it. Because honestly, I was only worried about you."

"You really think I give a shit about what your leg looked like? That I liked you for that?"

"No...but when everyone else does, or would, it's hard to make exceptions. I still can't believe you see me, the real me, rather than...someone else."

"I see you...I look at you every day, and never stop looking," Sveta replied, kissing her. "That's why I'm in love with you, too."

"What if that's not enough? I mean, for now it is, but what if you feel differently later on? That's what I'm scared of. I might never grow it back, Sveta. This might be it. And I'm cool with that...I don't want to be that girl anymore. I want you to love me like this."

"Then good, let's both be over it! Whatever happens, we won't regret what we lost. We're just freaks of nature. The losers left behind to love each other."

Helen laughed, and they kissed each other again and again. She could almost believe they would be happy now, even without the future she once planned, that everyone else in the world expected. She nuzzled against Sveta's cheek, kissed her neck, brushing the hair away so she could nibble her ear.

"Oh God! Sveta!" Helen exclaimed, almost leaping back.

"What? What?" Sveta said, catching her. "What's wrong?"

Helen's eyes were large, alive, frightened. Her hand flew to her mouth as she backed away. Sveta began feeling all over her face, trying to wipe away invisible bugs, when a finger grazed her ear. Or what used to be her ear. Its once-smooth surface was now furrowed and sharp. She felt it again and again, hoping it was just some trick of the moment, excitement and fear running rampant.

But no, it was there, and it had changed. She had changed. Part of her was horrified, wanting to rip off the offending ear. Another part was secretly relieved that she could still do it, after all. That she wasn't a lost cause like everyone (well, her mother) feared. Strangely, she had slept soundly for the past few nights without a single nightmare, as if she had finally made peace with her fear. Of course, she didn't want it for herself, her mother, or because of anything Malorie said; she wanted it for Helen, to prove to her that they could still be together. Maybe that's why her father had been able to do it so young, with so much of his life still ahead of him. Because he had a 'Helen' too.

"But I thought...you couldn't," Helen whispered.

"I can't! I mean, I couldn't! I have no idea how this happened. I guess...I don't know, I was scared to lose you, too."

"So you gave me the one thing I can't return," Helen said, with a laugh. "Well, Merry Christmas, Sveta! I got you the same thing."

"Thanks, it's just what I wanted," Sveta said.

She stumbled forward and fell into Helen's embrace, enveloped in tears and silence. Sveta's phone began vibrating again, a stream of texts from her mom, wondering where the hell she was and if she wanted to start walking home from now on? She returned it to her pocket, didn't care whether she walked home or stayed in this room for the rest of the night. She could only stare at Helen and remember that Keats poem about a lover chasing a nymph for all eternity, never catching her, always in the heat of pursuit. That's where she felt she was with Helen right now, and where they always would be; their fingers almost touching, their happiness real, but not of this earth.

"What do we do now?" Helen asked.

"Just hold me," Sveta said, closing her eyes. "Maybe if we stay here long enough, we'll fossilize into a *bas relief* so some modern-day Keats can write a poem about us. You know that poem...*beauty is truth, truth beauty,—that is all ye know on earth, and all ye need to know.*"

"You're such a show-off," Helen said, smiling. "Yeah, we read it in AP-English. But I think it's about an urn, and not a bas-whatever."

"Same difference. It's old, it's beautiful, it tells the truth."

"What truth?"

"Like Keats, we're going to live forever. And that's all I need to know."

See Joshua Grasso's story "Bas Relief" online at Metaphorosis.
If you liked it, leave a comment. Authors love that!

*Remember to subscribe to our e-mail updates so
you'll know when new stories are posted.*

About the story

"Bas Relief" was inspired by my experience teaching
college students, typically those fresh out of high
school. So many of them choose the same 2-3 majors,
have the same 2-3 goals, and almost all of them want
to become their parents (i.e., successful, big house,
vacations, etc.) as soon as possible. They don't seem
very excited about learning, or growing as a person, or
taking changes that might lead to unexpected
destinations. I kept thinking of them as young people
quickly turning into stone, desperate to plant
themselves into a suburban neighborhood as soon as
possible and have the accumulated wealth of the
world grow over them like moss. The more I thought
about it, the basic outline of the story suggested itself,
of teenagers who are pushed to 'change' as soon as
possible so they can take their places on the hill,
forming a man-made mountain of the 'haves' that look
down at the unfortunate 'have nots'. I originally meant
this to be satire, but as I started playing with the
characters, a love story suggested itself, since being
young is about finding love as much as finding
yourself. Indeed, your initial identity as a person is
often formed by how you want others to see you, and
how someone convinces you to see yourself (or
imagine yourself) because they believe in you. So I
wanted this story to be about more than satirizing
people who grow up too fast, and a society that makes
them; I also wanted it to be about how you decide to

open yourself to being in love when you're still at war with yourself, and how trust people to see the real 'you'.

A question for the author

Q: Do you use music for inspiration? If so, what do you listen to?

A: I honestly have trouble writing without music, since the right music unlocks the 'act' of writing itself. It's not that I need a soundtrack to my writing (since the music rarely completely matches what I'm trying to convey), but I need a piece that is sympathetic to either the mood I'm in at the time. Often, when I find the right piece of music, it can influence the writing and attach itself to a specific scene or character in unexpected ways. I'm a classical music nut, and have collected it seriously since I was about 17 (I'm in my 40's now), so I listen to everything from Bach to Mozart to Beethoven to Tchaikovsky to Stravinsky to Shostakovich and beyond. Orchestral music, in particular, seems to complement the act of writing since it's purely visual and emotional, yet without leading you down a specific alley the way music with words often do. You can put a favorite symphony on repeat and hear different stories each time, which is great, since writing requires you to come up with something new each time!

About the author

Joshua Grasso is a professor of English at a small university in Oklahoma, where he teaches classes in

British and World Literature, writing, and comics. He holds a PhD from Miami University where he specialized in 18th c. British Literature. When not teaching or writing, he enjoys hanging out with his two boys (one of whom is college bound!), reading everything he can get his hands on, and hunting for old vinyl and cds of classical music.

@JoshuaGrasso

An Hour in the City of Lightning

A.D. Guzman

The match flared orange and momentarily suffused crisp December air with an oddly soothing aroma of sulfur and smoke. Matt touched it to the end of his cigarette and inhaled deeply. Eyes closed, he exhaled a dragon-esque cloud and leaned against the church's brick wall.

"I thought you quit."

Matt cracked an eye and adjusted his glasses. His childhood confidant and cousin Renee stood beside him, one hand pressed to her lower back, the other supporting the weight of her eighth month of pregnancy. Thick, chestnut curls framed wide, impish green eyes and a crooked smile.

"I quit." Matt took another drag of his cigarette and tried to angle the smoke away from her. "But even a condemned man gets a last smoke before facing the firing squad."

"*Grandpa's* dead." Renee snatched the cigarette, then ground it out on the sidewalk. "*You're* just giving the eulogy in front of a bunch of grieving relatives."

Afternoon sun bathed them in a golden glow, though the winter chill worried its way through Matt's thin suit coat and dress slacks with annoying persistence. He rubbed his hands together and blew on them. A faint growl of thunder announced a storm cresting the northern horizon. A jagged line of lightning burned across the dark gray clouds.

"I'd rather face a firing squad," Matt confessed. "And Gran's been after me. Criticizing my hair, my clothes. Even my glasses are too 'hipster'. At least she's talking to me again, after my apparently unforgiveable sin of becoming a teacher instead of a doctor."

"I know Gran kind of pushed you away, but what about the rest of us? We've missed you. *I've* missed you." Renee paused and dropped her gaze to the slope of her belly. "Jim was laid off three months ago and things have been tough. You and Grandpa always knew what to say to make things right. But you practically disappeared. And now Grandpa."

Matt flinched. When the Gran who used to cut his grilled cheeses into perfect triangles declared his chosen profession a waste, it had stung. But the constant, offhanded digs at him and decreasingly subtle cold shoulder had built a distance between them that made Matt feel like a hostile intruder at family functions. Eventually, he'd stopped coming. Renee was right; he had disappeared on her.

Renee put a hand on his shoulder. "Gran only wants the best for you. You should cut her a little slack. She just lost her anchor of over sixty years. To lose the person that's been with you through *everything*, to have to handle that grief alone... Besides she wouldn't have chosen you to give the speech if she didn't think you'd do him proud."

"I'm not so sure of that." Matt pulled the slightly wrinkled print-out from his suit pocket. "She reduced my speech to a résumé of his accomplishments. There's nothing about the man Grandpa was."

Renee graciously allowed the change of subject. "Remember how he always hid our Christmas presents and made us follow clues to find them?"

Matt smiled. "I think he used that as an excuse to get us to do his chores."

They chuckled and watched the brewing storm toss bursts of light back and forth across the sky.

"He had a unique way of putting things," Matt said. "I remember he called each bolt of lightning a universe, born and extinguished in an instant, and thunder the cry of mourning. Although, get a few beers in him, then Grandpa swore up and down it was angels farting."

Renee wiped her eyes and choked out a laugh. "Grandpa sure could wax poetic when the mood struck. You're a lot like him, you know. You both love telling unusual stories."

"Then maybe I'll write a book of them."

"You'd better." Renee patted her belly. "This kid is going to need to know about his Great-Grandpa."

Matt threw his arm over her shoulders in a hug. "Well, we'd better get inside before they send a search party."

A loose nail made the lectern rock beneath Matt's nervous grip as he stood on the church's small stage beside his Grandpa's gleaming coffin. The sea of somber faces stared expectantly at him. Waiting. He ran a sweaty hand through his hair and shoved his glasses up the bridge of his nose. His freshman literature classes averaged over three hundred students, and he'd never had so much as a butterfly until now.

Renee rubbed her belly, discreetly flashing him a thumbs-up sign. Farther down, seated primly between Matt's father and Aunt Patrice, Gran dabbed her eyes with a lace hankie.

Matt looked at Gran's version of his speech, then deliberately folded it and slipped it back into his pocket next to an old velvet earring box Grandpa had given him. Gran's eyes widened behind her glasses and her hankie dropped forgotten to her lap. Her hand flew to the rose pendant she always wore for special occasions.

He cleared his throat and adjusted his tie. "Jeff Walters ... my grandpa. He ... um

... Well, it's hard to sum up a man. Impossible really. I mean, how can you encompass a person and their impact on the world in just a few words?

"We like closure. We like our laces tied, our ducks in a row, a pot of gold at the end of our rainbows. But the truth of the matter is that we're not threads in some cosmic tapestry that can be neatly trimmed and tied off when our part is complete. We're messy, wild, our influences unpredictable and often unintentional.

" 'We're like lightning,' Grandpa used to say. 'Bright, loud, dangerous. Brief but beautiful bursts of raw energy streaking through the world. For good or evil, our very existence alters the universe. And that's a damn big responsibility.'

"Which is exactly how Grandpa lived— though anyone who's ever seen him tinkering with his tractor can attest to that loud and dangerous bit." Matt grinned at the few bold enough to chuckle. "It's no surprise that Grandpa chose lightning as his analogy for life. His passion for the phenomenon is local legend. I don't think any of us will forget the Chicken Fiasco of '89." More laughter, louder this time.

"Grandpa was a man who saw magic in the mundane and potential in the most ordinary people. But what most of you might not know is why. When I was eleven, Grandpa took me camping and fishing for a weekend, just me and him. While we were on the lake, a good twenty minutes from where we'd put in, a storm swept in out of nowhere. A big monster with lots of rain and wind and lightning. I'd never seen Grandpa so excited. Those steel gray eyes mirrored the darkened sky. He tossed our rods into the bottom of the boat, told me to get down by his feet, started the motor and turned us back to shore.

"We bumped across the choppy water. Those twenty minutes it would take to get back seemed more like twenty hours. I stared up into a black, boiling maw with white lightning fangs behind us and knew it was hunting me.

"Grandpa must have noticed my fear, because he put on his story-telling grin and said, 'Awesome sight, ain't it, boy? There's a whole universe in there. In the lightning. That's what lightning is. Whole other worlds that're born, age and die in a split second. But they ain't lost; no energy ever is. It just ... changes. And who knows, maybe we're just a flash of lightning in some other universe too.'

" 'Nuh-uh,' I argued. 'Lightning is just a bunch of static electricity. We learned that in school.'

" 'Hogwash! I've been there, Matt. Spent an hour in the city of lightning. Any of your teachers or your books ever do that?'

"I shook my head. Then Grandpa cleared his throat and told me this story:

It was late summer, hotter'n hell and air so thick you could wring it out. I was seventeen, workin' the field for my Daddy, who'd been laid up by a kick from the mule. A storm blew in outta nowhere, a lot like this'un. I had just one more row to plow and decided to finish it out 'fore heading back to the house.

There was a deafening roar. It was the sound of the world tearin' apart, confusin' the senses. Noise blinded, light deafened. I tasted ozone, smelled 'lectricity. I could feel each'n every molecule of the air around me. I was livin' so hard I was dyin'.

Matt paused. He had a bad habit of speaking too fast when nervous. A baby in the back whimpered, precursor to a full-on wail. Its mother tossed a diaper bag over her shoulder and eased her way to the end of her row, flashing an apologetic

smile as everyone turned to watch her go.
Once the pair left, Matt took a deep breath
and went on, "Grandpa's distraction was
working. While I tried to figure out his
metaphors, I couldn't focus on the
weather chasing our little boat across the
lake. I said, 'That doesn't make sense,
Grandpa.'

"His tone became grave, and he turned
his steely eyes on me. 'You're a dreamer,
boy. More like me than your old man.' He
touched a finger to my chest. 'Keep lookin'
at the world with more'n your eyes, and
one day you'll understand.'

"I nodded, wide-eyed. Grandpa
continued with his tale:

When I came to my senses, the field was gone. I
was standin', naked as a jaybird, in the middle of a
crowded street. Like to died of embarrassment 'fore I
noticed that these weren't the kind of folks you
bump into down at the post office.

Their skin was a shiny black like that there
volcano stuff, with pale flecks that sparkled in the
purple sunlight. The texture was wrong, too, like they
really was made of rock or glass. Their eyes was
jewels. They didn't have no noses and not a strand of
hair.

Four long, skinny limbs like our arms an' legs
sprouted from short, stocky chests. Each hand only
had four fingers, two of 'em thumbs. They moved

funny, kinda like overgrown chickens 'cause their knee and elbow joints didn't bend like mine.

The city itself…well, looked somethin' like I'd imagine heaven to be. The buildings grew organic-like, more sculpture than architecture. Whatever material they used gave off white light that wiggled up into the violet sunlight like you see in them aurora things up north. I shaded my eyes from instinct more than pain—so much light shoulda blinded me, but I could see just fine.

A woman fell into step beside me. Don't ask me how I knew it was a woman; I just did. I smiled and asked, "Don't suppose you can tell me where I am?"

She brushed her fingertips 'cross the back of my hand. And I knew, like findin' a memory I'd forgot, that I was in Grown on Bay Rock, the capital of The Great Continent, the last settlement of the Children of the Third Sun. I was Visitor from Another Dimension and she wanted to know my name and the name of my Mother Sun.

"Name's Jeff," I told her. "From Texas. That's in the United States. It's a country on Earth."

Again, I knew her question when her fingers touched mine. "Earth is your sun?"

I shook my head. "No, it's my planet. The rock we live on."

She smiled and bluish streaks zigzagged 'cross her skin between them pale flecks, a thunderstorm in miniature. She touched a hand to her torso, then twined her fingers with mine. "I am One Who

Comes Third and Brings Happiness. I study the possibility of multiple dimensions and travel between them. Visitor from Another Dimension Jeff, you are proof of my theory. What is your purpose here?"

"My purpose?"

"You are an inter-dimensional envoy, yes? A representative of the Children of your sun?"

"No."

"A researcher like myself, then? A scientist?"

I laughed and slapped my knee. "Whoo-boy, have you got the wrong idea, lady. I'm just a simple farmer. I can read, write and figure well enough, but I don't know nothin' about other dimensions."

That odd skin-lightning returned, but this time it was more purple. "Then how did you come to be here, Visitor from Another Dimension Jeff?"

I shrugged. "Beats me. Best guess, my dang mule kicked me in the head and this is a dream."

"You must come from a less advanced world. I had not considered that possibility." Her skin flashed with mustard yellow streaks. I think she was a mite disappointed. "Well, if you dream, then let it be a good dream. Come, there is much to see before you wake."

It was the strangest sight-seeing tour I'd ever been on. I walked gardens of natural stone, though it don't seem right to call 'em stones, because each was as unique and beautiful as a snowflake. Some towered strong and mighty as oaks, others swept along the path, delicate as honeysuckle bushes, or clustered in little bunches like flowers.

One Who Comes Third and Brings Happiness explained that each stone took generations of gardeners thousands of years to grow. The occasional fountain of inky water filled the air with a pleasant tinkling. I couldn't smell a thing. Like walkin' through a garden in full bloom with a head cold. I guess without noses, they didn't have a sense of smell and didn't need their gardens to smell nice.

She took me to an art museum. Alien landscapes hung beside Picasso-like portraits. Irregular lumps of stone outnumbered the art, though. No painting or designs. Just big, ugly boulders on display. My guide went and put her hands all over one of 'em. Then she pulled me over and made me hug it, too. Now, I've never seen a museum that let you put your paws on the art, so I figured it had to be some kinda good luck charm. She explained that the artist's work was inside, not outside, for me to feel.

That threw me 'til I figured that if we had a sense of smell and they didn't, then maybe they got senses we don't. It embarrassed me, not bein' able to see this thing she was clearly so proud of. I asked if she'd describe it to me, and she touched her hand to mine ...

Matt paused to take a sip a from a convenient water bottle the funeral director had placed in the lectern. He was slipping into professor mode, a welcome reprieve from his previous nerves. His trained eye spotted a few people checking phones, but most were paying attention.

"Thunder clapped and the boat's engine sputtered out. We'd finally reached the dock, jostled against it by the waves, but all my attention was on Grandpa. 'What did you see, Grandpa? What was inside the rock?'

"He reached up and wiped his eyes. Rain poured down his face in tiny rivers, but for a second, I thought he might have been crying.

" 'I didn't see nothin'. But what I felt ...' His voice faltered. 'I just wish I could tell you, son. Imagine the very best day of your life stuck like a fly in amber, a perfect moment suspended for forever. And then do the same ten years later. It's the same moment, but not the same moment. The way when you're ten what you want most is a new bike, then ten years later it's a new car, then maybe ten years later a new house. The same want, just a different object. It was like that, Matt.'

"We grabbed our gear and scrambled for the cover of our cabin porch. Grandpa fixed us each a mug of cocoa, then continued:

I followed One Who Comes Third and Brings Happiness until my dogs were barkin'. Remember, I'd already been plowin' all day before getting zapped there. We saw their government and their churches to the Third Sun. We visited slums where coal-black bums, eyes milky and cracked, skin as dull and lifeless as real coal, huddled along the sidewalks.

She took me to the top of one of the towers. From the observation deck, I saw the city latticed below. Beyond, a pale, landscape, smooth as polished bone, curved around a harbor of inky water 'til it blended with the indigo horizon. That swollen purple sun shattered into millions of glitterin' shards against the sea. One Who Comes Third and Brings Happiness stood beside me, a melancholy green color sparkin' across her black skin.

She touched her hand to mine. "Our world is dying, Visitor from Another Dimension Jeff. What you see here is the decaying carcass of a once-vibrant society."

"But it's beautiful," I told her.

"Even Death has beauty after a fashion, but I would have you know our world as it once was."

I don't know how she did it, but suddenly I knew that place. I remembered its beginnin' and its histories. I knew its days of innocence, its awkward adolescence, the spectacle of its maturity up to that very moment, when it hobbled along in its final glory, leanin' on Death's tender shoulder. Didn't realize I was cryin' 'til I felt tears on my bare chest.

She touched my cheeks curiously and seemed to draw understandin' from my tears like she done from my hand. "Do not mourn us, Visitor from Another Dimension Jeff. Remember us. Everything ends, as it must, or there would be nothing new in the universe. But nothing is truly lost. It merely changes."

I think I fell in love with her a little, the way a boy falls a little in love with his kindergarten teacher, and I wanted to share somethin' of my world. It dawned on me then that in the entire time I'd been there, I hadn't seen so much as a leaf, a stick or a tuft of grass. So I grabbed her hand and tried to give her what I'd give any girl I wanted to impress—a flower. I thought about the most perfect blossom I'd ever laid eyes on. I thought about the satiny texture of the petals, the fragrance, the color, the shape, and the joy I'd felt after seein' this result of my hard work.

When I opened my eyes, she had one hand pressed over her torso where I guessed her heart was and a steady pulsing rainbow of sparks washed across her black skin. Didn't take much intuition to figure she was cryin', too.

She extended her hand, a flat stone the size of a quarter gripped between both thumbs.

"Even if only as a dream, something of this place will endure. It has been a unique pleasure to spend this hour with you."

Then she took my hand, nestled the stone onto my palm and folded my fingers closed over it, like a mama swaddlin' her babe. I swallowed around a knot in my throat. I might not have been a scientist or explorer, but I was a farmer. And I knew exactly what to do with a seed.

Matt paused. The church was silent; even the sniffling had stopped. Most leaned forward in their seats, attentive; but some resembled the Math and Science majors in his freshman English class. He risked a look at Gran, expecting wrath. Instead, she clutched that rose so hard her knuckles went white, a hint of a smile on her face even as tears and snot dripped freely. She held his gaze, then deliberately mouthed, "Thank you."

Maybe asking him to do the speech had been a kind of olive branch, and changing it was her way of pushing him to do exactly what he'd done: give a spontaneous, heartfelt tribute to the man they all loved. Tears burning his own eyes, Matt dipped his head to her in acceptance of this chance for reconciliation.

"Grandpa had been struck by lightning while working in the field. He came to with his mother wailing over him, but suffered nothing worse than a couple of minor burns. Now, the odds of being struck by lightning are better than your chances of ever meeting another man as wonderful as him. He might not have changed the world, but he changed the way a good number of us perceive it."

Matt stuck his hand in his jacket pocket and grasped the velvet box. "A single story hardly feels adequate to fill the void left by Grandpa's death, but we can take comfort in knowing that even if only as a story, something of him endures. That we *are* a lot like lightning. Our very existence alters the universe. And no one is truly lost when they've changed those left behind."

The graveside service was unpleasantly chilly. A stiff afternoon breeze had kicked up and dropped the temperature close to freezing. Matt stood, huddled in his coat, between Bill the bait shop guy and Grandpa's mechanic as he waited his turn to pay his last respects.

Renee waddled to his side, her chestnut curls bobbing and weaving drunkenly in the wind, a white rose clutched in her hand. "Now you definitely have to write that book. I don't think I've ever seen Gran cry like that. I saw you two hug and make up earlier, too. Does that mean you'll come to the family luncheon?"

She tried to play it casual, but Matt could tell by the way she bit her lip and picked at her fingernails that his answer really mattered to her. Things must have been worse than she'd let on before. He'd noticed her husband Jim's absence. "Wouldn't miss it," he assured her. "We've got a lot of catching up to do."

Renee turned so he wouldn't see her relief, so Matt pretended not to notice. Bill said a quick prayer over the coffin, then Matt and Renee were next. They stepped forward and Renee dropped the rose onto the lid. They shuffled on until they stood a short distance from the gathered mourners.

"So," Renee spoke in a semi-whisper. "Did Grandpa really get struck by lightning?"

Matt nodded.

"Then that story, I mean, he had like brain damage or something, right?" Renee pressed. "A hallucination. Although knowing Grandpa, he might have just made the whole thing up."

"I guess anything's possible, but ..." Matt pulled the box from his pocket and caressed the velvety exterior, the same as he'd done so many years ago out on that lake. "Grandpa told that story and passed this on to a frightened boy who was looking for reassurance in a storm. I think yours is a different kind of storm, but you're scared and looking for reassurance, too." He took Renee's hand and planted the box firmly in her palm, folding her fingers over it.

She gazed up at him, her expression mildly puzzled, then lifted the lid. Matt couldn't see the quarter-sized stone nestled inside from this angle, but he caught the rainbow reflection in Renee's eyes as that mysterious light pulsed across the stone's surface. Renee gasped and clutched the box to her chest. "Is this...? It isn't just some story?"

"It's a reminder. Even if only as a story, something of that place endures. Something of Grandpa endures." With a conspiratorial wink, Matt gestured at her belly, leaned close to her ear and whispered, "And we will always be there to help you through the storm."

See A.D. Guzman's story "An Hour in the City of Lightning" online at Metaphorosis.
If you liked it, leave a comment. Authors love that!
Remember to subscribe to our e-mail updates so you'll know when new stories are posted.

About the story

"An Hour in the City of Lightning" began with my grandmother literally kicking me and my kids and my father out when we showed up at her house to sit a bedside vigil for my dying grandfather because, according to her, we weren't family. And a fascinating documentary about how awesome lightning is! Angry and hurt, I vented those feelings into a story where I could properly say goodbye to my grandfather and transform that hurt into something beautiful and wonderful. Now that time has passed, I was able to purge that initial anger and keep the beautiful celebration of how "no one is truly lost when they've changed those left behind."

The characters are, of course, not my family. My grandfather was a respected lawyer and judge, not a farmer, but he was a loveable, jolly man who slapped tunes for us grandkids on his false leg (he lost it in WWII) and invented funny nicknames for the people in his life. My nickname was Little Mandidty Went to the

City and Played a Ditty. My favorite was his proctologist Dr. Roe, or as he called him, Dr. Row, Row, Row Your Bottom. I borrowed his humor and kindness for the grandpa character. In fairness to my grandmother, she adopted my mother as a child so we were only family on paper not by blood. And I've come to think a lot of her traits that I borrowed for Gran were probably the result of being a very ambitious woman living in a time and place with few opportunities for a woman to achieve respect and authority for herself.

The lightning documentary did not imply that there are other worlds inside lightning, but rather, it showed footage of how lightning decides where to strike, following stepped leaders branching and dissipating faster than the eye can see until that perfect connection is made. This reminded me of multiverse theories, of realities branching off, and thus the City of Lightning was born. I've never ventured beyond our universe myself, but I hold out hope that there is a myriad of strange and wonderful worlds out there to be discovered. And that we'll give them the respect they deserve when we do.

A question for the author

Q: If someone wanted to make an animated series out of your work, based on the title or recurring themes, what would it look like?

A: I love this question because I often picture my story as a movie or animation as I'm writing. For "An Hour in the City of Lightning" I totally see something in the style of Miyazaki's *Howl's Moving Castle* or *Castle in the Sky*. Studio Ghibli has a beautiful and honest way of bringing the most mundane and extraordinary characters to life, side by side in the same or parallel universes, so I would love to see my characters represented that way. Also, the worldbuilding in Miyazaki's animation shows a love and respect for nature and depicts strange worlds as places equally as complex, beautiful, dangerous, and real as our own, which I feel aligns with the dual dimensions and themes of my story.

About the author

A.D. Guzman is a writer of speculative fiction and all-around lover of story. She earned a Bachelor of Arts in English from Texas A&M Commerce. She taught adult ESL for fourteen years and preschool Spanish for eight. Now, she coordinates Wills Point Veterinary Clinic's online store, dabbles in payroll and serves as occasional, unofficial IT support. She serves as Membership Chair on the Friends of Riter C. Hulsey Public Library board, proudly producing amusing and informative promotional materials. She's a hobby bird photographer and, if you like birds and/or fantasy, she has some acrylic and watercolor pieces you'll love. She runs, does yoga, bikes, hikes, pretty much anything active and outdoors. She lives in Texas with her husband, two wonderful adult kids, four finches, three parakeets, a cat, and a snake.

adguzmanwrites.com, @AD_Guzman00

Infinite Possibilities

Michael Gardner

A mystery USB leads Adrian to a cabin where he finds a book written by himself. The book contains schematics for a machine. Adrian, being good with his hands, starts to build.

Adrian receives a second USB. It contains video proof that his wife, Candice, is having an affair. Distraught, Adrian returns to the cabin. The television inside turns on, reveals Other Adrian. Other Adrian explains he is from a parallel world. His life's work is locating other versions of himself, bringing them across to his world where they share knowledge and unlock the mysteries of the universe. Other Adrian needs Adrian to build the machine to bring him across.

Later, Adrian receives an email from Other Adrian's agent asking to meet.

3

He's chosen one of the coffee places in the city that Candice talks about. A place on the corner of a pedestrian mall, and a busy road. It's newly painted, polished concrete floors, a strange assortment of furniture—some old, some new—which Adrian senses is less random and more planned than appears at first glance.

He takes a table outside, in the mall. It isn't the nicest table. The drone of cars from the nearby road is prevalent. As is the scent of tar and exhaust, which overpowers the smell of coffee. But he wants to be outside, to have a view of his contact when they arrive. Deep down, he's also wondering if Candice might drop by, catch him out with someone, realise he's got secrets too. Why else has he picked a cafe that she talks about? But then again, when was the last time she mentioned this place? A month ago? More? He doesn't know. If he's honest, he doesn't really listen anymore. Is that why she looks elsewhere? No, that's on her, not him.

He watches pedestrians approach in twos, in threes, more. Some stop, survey the menu, others walk on. The breeze is picking up, but it's warm out, even as the sun sinks low in the sky.

When the waiter approaches, he orders a cappuccino to get rid of him. That's when he sees her.

Taylor Bradbury. The expat he met in Thailand. That forced herself into his and Candice's world. That convinced Candice to share him. That rocked his world, then left. And even though he didn't want to think of her over the years, he has, often.

Seeing her now, he recalls the feel of her velvet, red hair across his chest. Like a phantom limb. He swallows, shrinks in his chair. He simultaneously wants to talk to her, and to sneak away.

She's talking to the waiter, who turns and points at Adrian, and she looks, catches his eye, and he hers, and it's too late to go. He jerks upright, clears his throat. She smiles, walks toward him. He can't bring himself to smile back.

She slides into the chair across from him, places her handbag on the ground, leans forward, and his eyes are drawn to the shock of red hair that slides half across her left eye, and the pale freckled skin of her cheek. In his mind, he knows those freckles continue down her chest, and her stomach. He swallows again.

"Long time," she says. There's a huskiness in her voice he doesn't remember. Experience, age. A change that makes her more attractive.

"I thought I was getting answers, not more..." He shrugs, gives some sort of weak hand wave.

"Questions? Maybe I bring both," she says, laughs. She leans back into her chair, casual. A shadow tells him someone else is close, and he looks up to see a man backlit by the sun. He blinks twice, and the image resolves into a waiter carrying his coffee. The man places it in front of him.

"Anything else?" the waiter asks.

"You have anything harder than this?" Taylor says.

"We have an assortment of wines and beers. Would you like to see a menu?"

"No. Just bring me a pale ale if you have one?"

Adrian holds up two fingers. "Two, please," he says.

The waiter nods. Then he's gone.

Adrian watches Taylor watch him wrestle with all of this. He forces a smile. "So…" he says.

"I took the videos. I dropped off the USBs. I—"

"You're his agent."

She hesitates a beat. "Your agent."

"No. That's not me. That's…" But how does he finish?

She reaches out and places a hand on his. Electricity sizzles across his skin. Heat. He snatches his hand back.

"I work as a historian for the Council," she says, as if that explain things. He feels his face bunch in confusion. She hurries on. "My team is responsible for documenting, restoring and maintaining local historical sites."

"Like the cabin," he says.

"Like the cabin," she repeats.

The waiter reappears with a tray, two beers—a craft beer that Adrian doesn't recognise—two glasses. Adrian holds his tongue as the waiter places a bottle in front of Taylor, and then another in front of him. They clink pleasantly against the glass-topped table. He deposits the glasses, then dissolves back into the cafe throng without offering to pour their drinks.

Taylor pours her beer into the glass. Adrian grabs the bottle and takes a long draw. It's achingly cold, bitter. When he places the half empty bottle back on the table, Taylor is looking at him with a grin. She raises her glass, "Cheers," she says, takes a sip.

After she swallows, she continues. "The furniture appeared one day. The TV, the rug, the armchair."

"Someone moved it in? Someone else? Another agent maybe?"

She shakes her head, no. She seems certain. "The cabin was being restored. We had the fences in place, and the gate was locked each night. There was no sign that the fence or lock had been tampered with, and yet one day the cabin was empty, the next..."

"Not," he offers.

She takes another sip of beer. It's familiar, he thinks, the way she licks her top lip after. Déjà vu.

"We removed it, paid a company to dispose of it. Then it happened again. I was alone when I found it the second time. I dropped by the site on my way to the office, I can't even remember why. Remeasuring the beam we were repairing, maybe? Anyway, it was back. What looked like the same TV. The same rug. The same armchair and side table and TV stand. As well as a book."

"By me."

"Yes, by you. Then you were there. On the screen. And so was I."

"You were on the screen as well?"

She nods. "Never at the same time. It would switch from you to me."

"Other Adrian."

"Pardon?"

"That's what I call him."

She nods at this, like she approves.

"I've never seen you," he says.

"No, Other Adrian said it wouldn't help. Not when I explained our brief interaction."

"You told him about Thailand?"

"Not in detail, but the gist of it. The brevity of our time together. Have you been reading your book?"

Adrian pauses a beat, nods. "Some. Infinite worlds with infinite possibilities."

She shrugs. "Other Adrian says that is not strictly true. The infinite possibilities part, that is. Some things are always drawn together. It happens over and over again, like electrons orbiting a nucleus. They may stray, but the attraction remains. In this possibility, you've strayed."

Adrian feels hot, sweaty. Taylor seems clearer than clear, realer than real. "What does that mean?" he asks.

"Other Adrian and Other Taylor, they're together in their world, and most others they find. They're doing this together. Bringing other versions of them—of us— together. Joining our experiences to crack open the skull of the universe, to look inside at the grey matter, to learn it all."

Like finding a god and destroying her, he thinks. He shivers despite the heat. She reaches toward him again, hesitates. When he keeps his hand on the table, she lowers hers, places it on his. This time he maintains contact, allows the heat of her skin to spark a fire inside him and send embers into his bloodstream, into his pounding heart, into his brain.

"Thailand was meant to happen," she says, her voice a soft rasp. "This was meant to happen."

His hand is shaking under hers. He feels desire. A want. He doesn't trust himself. He gently untangles his hand from hers, stands.

"I'm sorry," he says. "I can't... I'm sorry."

He turns to leave, but stops when she speaks. "I can show you where Candice is now. Whom she is with. What she is doing."

He swallows. He wills himself to leave. But he can't. He turns back toward Taylor's intense flame, sits. "I'm not sure I want that."

She sighs with sympathy. "I know. But it's necessary."

And he understands that it is. He won't be able to move forward without it. He nods, and Taylor calls for the bill.

He was thirty-six when his appendix burst. The pain had built steadily over several days, a burning sensation that he at first mistook for indigestion. But it became sharper, focused. A throbbing low in his right side that felt like a nail had been hammered into his gut when he applied pressure. In hindsight, he was naive. He thought it was his diet, or drinking too much. He'd continued driving the bus as the pain had built, then the fever, hoping it'd all go away.

It was Candice that twigged to what was going on. Which was odd in hindsight. They weren't talking much at the time. She was grieving her mother and after some clumsy efforts by Adrian to provide comfort, she made clear there was nothing he could do to make it better. So, he gave her space. And at the same time started to resent her for going back on the pill without a discussion.

Despite that, she must have intuited something was wrong with him, because she broke through, and somehow deduced what was happening. When she said the word appendix, it was like watching an old silent film where a lightbulb turns on above the main character's head.

By the time he got to the hospital, he felt better. The pressure in his right side had reached a crescendo and suddenly, like jumping from a plane, he felt weightless, he felt relief. They told him after that that was the moment it ruptured.

He doesn't remember much about going into surgery. An anaesthetist that asked him if he was nervous, his replying no, all the while the heart monitor pinging like a slot machine revealing his lie. He remembers lights, counting backward, then… he was awake.

It was all over, but he didn't realise at first. He didn't realise much of anything, other than that there was a presence next to him, slumped in a hard armchair.

"Mum?" he asked, surprised at how sluggish his words sounded. He could see he was in a hospital, but in those first few moments, he wasn't sure why. "Mum?" he said again.

A hand reached out, grasped his. Young skin. Maybe not as young as it once was, but warm, soft. The first time Candice had touched him in months. Or maybe, if he were honest, the first time he'd allowed her touch to get through the shell he'd erected. And maybe then only because of the morphine that fogged his senses, that made him confused about what was going on.

"It's me, babe," came the weary reply. He forced himself to look her over, to take her in. She'd just woken, but even in his daze, he could see she was exhausted.

"Did you stay here all night?" he asked in that slow, unfamiliar drawl. His mouth felt so dry.

As if intuiting this, she held out a cup for him, helped him sip it. When he was done, he sighed and sat back against his pillows.

"Don't worry about me," she'd said, smiling. "Get some sleep."

And he had. It had been easy to sink back into oblivion, to let the drugs wash his mind clean. But before he went to sleep, a thought struck him. Stuck with him. Would I have done that for her? He didn't know. But something about that act, that willingness to put aside her comfort just to make sure he had someone familiar nearby when he woke in a drugged daze, half confused, that struck him as something amazing.

Adrian and Taylor stand across the road from the apartment building that Adrian last saw on video. The apartment building that his wife disappeared into with a strange man.

"She comes here at least once a week, sometimes more," Taylor says. Adrian deduces that she's been following his wife for some time. A conclusion that seems important, but he's too distracted to give it much attention.

"She's there now?" he asks, staring across the road. It's still light out, but only just. The sun has sunk most of the way beneath the horizon, and the sky has faded from blue to grey.

"Yes."

He sees the man again in his mind. The tall man, with dark hair, in the nice suit. A success, unlike him. He swallows, notices the sweat in his armpits spreading like spilt ink on paper.

"His apartment is on the third floor. I know which one," Taylor says. He looks at her, sees a sparkle in her eye. She appears to be enjoying herself. His face tightens into a frown. As he looks back across the road the street lights shimmer to life, one after the other.

"They deserve to be caught, to be screamed at, to..." Taylor leaves the thought hanging. His mind takes it, runs with it. He imagines kicking in a door, yelling. It doesn't feel right. Just as quickly, he imagines stumbling into a bedroom that smells of sweat and sex, losing his words, his anger replaced with embarrassment. He imagines himself apologising, and he feels his face redden. He swallows again. "No," he says, barely a whisper. "No, I don't think so. I don't want to see... I don't—"

"I understand," Taylor interjects, and takes his clammy hand in her soft, dry one. She rubs the back of it, ever so gently, with her thumb. A thumb that is small, and smooth, and sensual. Adrian's eyes are drawn to it, watching it move back and forth. Slowly, very slowly, his eyes move up her pale arm, to her shoulder, to her face, and her green eyes looking back at him. They sparkle with a want.

She licks her lips. They look so red, ripe. "We could get another drink? Or...?"

His hand tingles, his stomach flutters. He shakes his head, unwinds his hand from hers. "No, not tonight. I just want to go home." He hates the sound of defeat in his voice.

"Not tonight?" she asks.

He's married. He should make clear he means not ever. But he doesn't. He leaves that door open. "I've got more work to do on the machine."

She smiles. "Okay, then. A raincheck."

Adrian stares at the maze of wires and circuits in the machine. His eyesight is strained, his hair is greasy, and he can smell his own body odour. He's exhausted, and he just wants to leave the garage and take a shower, but he can't, not yet.

He's followed the instructions in the book, and yet the machine does nothing. Not that the book really explains what it is supposed to do, but he knows that the nothing it is currently doing is not right. There should be a hum of electricity when he switches it on, a vibration of power, heat. But there's nothing, and he's certain he's made an error in the construction. A loose wire, a faulty connection. Yet he can't seem to locate the problem.

He's so tired he's having trouble seeing straight. But he can't let this go. So he stares into the casing, into the circuitry, into the jungle of wiring. There's something comforting about the trance he's in, as unfathomable and impenetrable as it is.

The loud groan of the garage door rising jerks him from his stupor. He turns, squints as bright sunlight assaults his eyes. Morning already? he thinks. He sees bare feet, legs, a short skirt, shoes held in a slender hand. She's been out all night, he realises, while he has been here working.

She doesn't see him at first. It gives him time to appraise her. A ruffled top, make-up smeared, hair frazzled. He wants to despise her, but instead the usual cocktail of confused emotions emerges. Lust, love, a deep, throbbing pain like an infected tooth.

He clears his throat, and her head jerks toward him, her eyes widen with surprise. "Adrian?" she says. "You're up early."

She stands on the periphery of the garage, frozen.

He blinks. It feels like slow motion. He nods toward the machine as if that explains it.

"Oh," she says. She takes two hesitant steps into the garage, stops. "Have you finished?"

"Where were you?" he asks. His voice sounds strange in his ears, feels strange leaving his mouth. It's like listening to someone else, someone emotionless. A bluff, because his emotions are a pit of seething snakes, constricting, biting, slithering all over one another.

"Out," she says too loudly. Her eyes dart away. "With Jenny and the girls, like I said." She glances back at him.

"All night? Or you slept it off at Jenny's place."

Candice swallows, which sounds loud contrasted with the quiet of the early morning. "I stayed with Jenny, of course."

"Like last weekend," he says.

She straightens, places both hands on her hips, the right still holding her shoes. "Yes, like last weekend. What did you think I was doing?" she says, on the offensive now. His body responds like it always does. His stomach dives down to his toes, his neck warms, his heart beats harder. He's a chastened child, being told off in front of the class. He hates this feeling. Hates that she knows she can do this to him, turn on him and make him feel apologetic for her behaviour.

He licks his lips. They're dry, and his tongue does little to moisten them. He tries to hold her gaze, but he can't. He lowers his eyes, shakes his head in a half apology.

She continues to glower for a few beats, then she moves toward the door into the house, her bare feet padding softly against the cement.

His words surprise him as much as her. "Who is he?"

She freezes. He regards her curiously, waits. He's nervous, and yet he also feels removed from his physical body, watching everything from a safe distance.

She turns slowly, purses her lips, huffs. "So that's what you think of me. A whore? Or are you just jealous, once again, that I have a life? That I refuse to give up, and wallow at home every weekend with you feeling sorry for myself? Is that it?"

He opens his mouth to respond, but she doesn't let him.

"I was out with Jenny. Understood? I keep telling you that you can come out with us anytime you like. It's you that chooses not to. So you don't get the right to start throwing wild accusations around just because you've let your imagination run away with you."

He rises from his seat, the stool screeching as it slides over the concrete.

"No, don't fucking come near me. I'm getting a shower, and having a sleep. You could do with the same. You stink. But do me a favour, take the spare room."

She turns to go, and he's suddenly overwhelmed by the unfairness of it all.

His heart turns to fire. His churning belly hardens into stone and he feels his face contort into something bitter. "Twenty-six Charlton Street," Adrian hisses.

She stutters mid-stride, deflates before his eyes. When she looks back her mouth is an 'o', and her eyes are glassy with a hint of tears. Adrian thinks she will continue to deny what he knows. Thinks she will attack him again. But she doesn't. She turns, and rushes into the house.

He wakes with a start, confused, hot, disoriented. Bright sunlight penetrates the room through flimsy curtains. A room that isn't his. This one has pale grey walls, and a musty smell. A linen doona covers him. Then it hits him. His accusation, Candice's reaction, his nap in the spare room.

He throws the covers back, sits up on the edge of the bed. Everything feels different. Like he went to sleep Adrian, and woke up someone else. The room feels on the edge of eruption. A build-up of electricity. A dam holding a torrent of water back. He feels dizzy, and he clings hard to the bed as if this might keep him from falling. He closes his eyes, opens them. The dizziness recedes.

He rises, eases the door open, pokes a head out. It's quiet. The house is steeped in it. Not a silence of emptiness, but something else. A full silence. Filled with words yet to be said. He knows Candice is in their room, sleeping or feigning sleep. Right now, he doesn't care. That she's here, or for her words. He doesn't need to do this her way. He doesn't need to listen. He's shared his knowledge. Now he can act. Move on. But to where? His mind wanders to Taylor, to the machine, to the cabin.

He moves out of the bedroom, walks as quietly as he can into the living/dining/kitchen space. He's still wearing the clothes he worked through the night in. They're crumpled, and smell of stale sweat.

In the kitchen he checks the clock on the microwave, sees that it's just after eleven am. He hasn't slept long. He thinks about turning the kettle on, but then thinks better of it. He doesn't want to rouse her. He wants this moment to himself. The eye of the storm. He removes orange juice from the fridge, quietly pours a glass, and sits at the bench to drink.

He spies his phone on the charger, removes it, checks for messages, none, emails, one. He opens it and there she is. Redhead22. The only thing she's sent is a phone number. He checks the hall again as if he might find Candice lurking there, then dials. As it rings, he gets up and goes to the garage, closes the door behind him. She answers.

"I was wondering when you'd call," she says. Her voice is husky, sensual.

Adrian swallows. "When I'd call? Not if?"

"I'm an optimist." He can hear the smile in her words. She's enjoying this, he thinks. "How did she take it?" she asks.

He wonders how she knew he'd confront her. "Like Candice."

"What's that mean?"

He shakes his head. Like it's my fault, he thinks. He wonders for the briefest moment whether it might be, but then corrects himself. No. It's not. It's hers. What has he ever done but be faithful? And yet there's guilt there. Something that gnaws at him, which he pushes down, ignores for now. "It means she took it badly, but that doesn't matter. I've nearly finished the machine."

"Oh?" she says, both like this is a surprise and expected at the same time. "So you've decided? You'll be brought across? To join him? To join us?" There's an eagerness in her tone.

"I'd like to speak to him again first," he says.

"Of course."

"And I won't do it alone."

"You won't have to. I'll be there."

He swallows again. In his mind he dips into the past and feels, vividly, her soft hands. He sees the pale skin of her arm as it caresses his chest. He can feel the swell of her breasts against him. He shivers. She said they were made for each other. It's inevitable. A repeated attraction across infinite worlds. He feels it.

"Do you have a car?" he asks.

"Yes, of course."

"Will you come get me when I'm finished?"

"Yes," she whispers into the phone. "I will."

"Taylor?"

"Yes, Adrian." He wants to thank her for finding him. He wants to explain his excitement, his curiosity, his fear, his guilt. Yet the words avoid his grasp. "I'll call again soon."

She hangs up. He stares at the dormant phone in his hand for a moment, then he goes to his workbench, and feeling fresher, he begins to recheck the wiring.

He finishes soldering, places the iron on the bench, stretches his neck left, right. It clicks loudly, he grimaces, rolls his shoulders.

He takes a breath, switches the machine on, waits for a hum of electricity, waits for something, anything to happen.

Nothing.

His shoulders slump. He flips the power switch off, then on. Nothing. Off again.

The door to the house opens. He looks and finds Candice standing in the doorframe, hands on hips, pouting. "Okay, I'm sorry. You caught me, and I'm sorry."

He stares, wants to say something, can't.

She steps into the garage, continues. "It didn't mean anything. Nothing. It... I..." As he watches, she appears to shrink into herself. She takes a couple more hesitant steps, stops. Her voice is softer when she speaks. "I didn't want this. Not really. It's just... We..."

He sees tears in her eyes. One spills onto her cheek, and leaves a silvery trail as it runs toward her chin. Part of him feels sorry for her. Another part observes from afar, detached.

"It's been so long," she whispers, and yet he hears her voice clearly across the garage. "So long since you looked at me like I was... new. Lovely."

She sniffs. He feels the pull of the machine, the temptation to turn and work again on its faults, and yet her gravity also draws him.

"His name is John. He made me feel special. I haven't felt like that since we met. And... it's no excuse, I know, but I wanted to recapture what we had once. Just for a time."

She falls into a deep silence, looks at her feet. Waits. He can't help but stare at her. She's pitiful and untrustworthy, he tells himself. From outside comes the sounds of birdsong, and a dog barking a few streets away.

"Okay. Fine," he mutters. "Now leave me alone."

She looks at him then as if he's a bug she'd like to bring her boot down on. She looks at him as if he's the one that's been caught fucking someone else. He should be angry, but he's not. He's tired of this one-sided discussion. But he can see there's more.

"You get what I'm saying, don't you?" she asks, her voice rising. "This is your fault. Your fucking fault." She glowers. "I married someone else. Someone exciting. Then he changed. Into you. I just want my Adrian back. Not this fucking tranquilized, no ambition, emotionally bereft person you've become. I wanted to feel something, Adrian. Anything. That's why I cheated, you bastard." She's screaming now. Red faced, arms gesticulating, breathing hard.

Adrian sighs, turns away and refocuses on the machine. He flinches when Candice screams. A wail that rises until his ears hurt, and he has to cover them with both hands. After, silence. He drops his hands, and hears only Candice's harsh breathing.

He turns to her. Looks at her purple, angry face. "I have work to do," he says quietly.

She looks like she will explode. Opens her mouth, closes it. Opens it again. "With that machine?" she screeches. "With that fucking game. Why? What's so important?"

"You told me I needed something like this in my life," he says, knowing that she doesn't know that the game is real, that something big is at stake. He stares at her, and she at him. He doesn't feel the guilt anymore, or the obligation. She's broken all of that. He turns back to the machine and picks up the soldering iron. He waits for her to yell again, but she doesn't. Instead, he hears her footsteps as she moves back into the house. It makes him feel larger, bolder. If he can just find this faulty wire, he thinks. He resumes his work.

Twelve months back, Adrian relented and went out with Candice and her friends. They all met up at an Italian restaurant in the city with nice food, and nicer wine. He doesn't recall the name of the place, but he remembers the exposed brick, the smoky scent of the wood fired pizza oven, the buzz of wait staff floating between patrons.

They were given a large table along one wall of the restaurant. He sat on the bench against the wall next to Candice.

He was struck that night by her people. In a few short years, they'd all changed. He didn't know any of them. The only topics they talked about were the office, difficult clients, and clever solutions. They used jargon that made discussions hard to follow. Whole sentences floated by him.

He presumed most of them worked with Candice—colleagues, bosses, and managers once removed. Important people, comfortable in their own spheres. People who'd shrunk the world down to a bubble small enough to understand and beat. A bubble that contained accounting, a firm of a few hundred people, and a list of clients. Beyond that, nothing of importance.

The thing was, from the perspective of an outsider—and a lowly bus driver who didn't define himself by his meagre contribution to society at that—the stream of words was both impressive and thin. Like discovering the new town you've entered is actually a movie set with nothing but scaffolding behind the colourful facade.

These people only seemed to have two settings: talk, or wait to talk. And for all of the fancy words, the topics were always about whomever was the speaker at the time.

Yet that night sticks in his mind. On one level, Candice mimicked them, and he listened to her with the same detached and horrified fascination as he did the others. But when someone else took centre stage, she'd place her hand on his knee under the table, lean close to him until her hair ticked his ear, the side of his neck. Sometimes she'd sneak a kiss. A quick peck on his cheek, occasionally something that lingered longer, a nibble at the corner of his mouth. She'd lean in and whisper real words to him. She thanked him a lot. Told him she loved him. Told him she couldn't have got where she was without him.

That night he saw her. Not the pantomime she produced for work. Not the judgement at home. Her. The girl he'd first met and fallen for. It was like she'd lifted the window a crack to let in fresh air, and through it he'd caught the scent of her, a flash of the real her walking by.

That night he realised that behind their difficulties, if he could just peel back the layers enough, he'd find her still there. Someone pure and familiar. He just had to try.

But it was easy to fall back into old habits, and familiar patterns. Adrian promised to try, but he put it off to next week, then the week after, then eventually he stopped promising. And she didn't reveal herself again.

It's hot in the garage. Adrian's sweating, beads running freely down his back, his chest. His armpits are dark, wet, and the heady stink of him is in his nostrils. There's also the scent of solder in the air, sharp and biting. One more try, he thinks. He turns on the power.

At first, nothing changes. But then he notices a subtle increase in heat, and hears the soft, resonant hum of electricity coursing through wires. He smiles so broadly his cheeks hurt. He's finally done it.

Carefully, he swings the top steel panel back into place. As it clicks together, he feels the machine vibrate under his hands, so subtly he might not have noticed if he weren't touching the casing. The hairs on his arm rise. He feels something in his spine do the same, then his brain. He suddenly feels naked. Like a monstrous eye has opened and turned toward him. He feels small, inconsequential under that gaze. He pulls his hands away like he's been stung, flips the power off. The hum dies, the vibrations cease, and he feels himself again. He puts it down to working too hard without enough sleep.

He takes out his phone, calls Taylor.

"Did you fix it?" she asks, excitedly.

"I fixed it," he says.

She makes a sound that makes him think of sex and sweat. A sound she might have made in bed with him all those years ago. He swallows hard.

"I'll be there in twenty minutes."

"Wait," he says, and for a moment he's not sure if he's caught her before she's hung up. Then he hears her breathing.

"For what?"

"You're really sure about this? You're ready to just leave this world behind on the promises of a stranger? What if it's a trick? What if it's not what he promised?" He can't shake the feeling that this is all

too big, too crazy, and important. He
doesn't seem to have enough information
to make an informed decision. He feels his
emotions are running too high. That
someone may be coercing him into
something that he shouldn't do.

"I didn't talk to a stranger," she says
matter-of-factly. "I spoke to me. Then I
spoke to you."

Other Adrian isn't him, he thinks.

"If you can't trust yourself, whom can
you trust?" she says. "And besides, what's
here for me that's so great?"

He hesitates, thinking. "Okay," he says
eventually. "But give me half an hour. I
desperately need a shower."

"Half an hour it is." He can hear the
smile in her voice.

Candice is waiting when he steps out of
the bathroom, hair wet, a towel wrapped
around his waist. She looks like she's
been crying, and her arms are crossed
defensively across her chest.

He stops, stares, waits.

"Can we talk?" she says. Her voice is
soft, raspy. He feels for her briefly, until

he recalls what she did. This isn't his fault.

"I don't have time," he says. He steps past her, and walks to their bedroom. He doesn't know what he should wear, or what he should bring. Candice follows him into the room. He ignores her, removes clean underwear from his drawer, puts them on without removing the towel.

"I want to explain," she says, watching him as he opens the wardrobe. He rifles through his shirts, eventually picks a plain, white tee, throws it over his head.

"I miss you," she says.

He regards her quizzically, turns back to the wardrobe, finds a pair of black chinos. "Well, I'm always here," he says, not looking.

"But you're not," she says.

He hesitates, drops the towel and steps into his pants.

"You haven't been for a long time," she continues. "I feel like you've disappeared into yourself. You've anesthetised the vibrant parts of you."

He shoots her a glare, opens his mouth to say something, but then can't bring himself to fight. He swings the wardrobe door open wider. There's a mirror affixed to the inside. He runs a hand through his wet hair. He can see her in the reflection, eyes on his back. Sad eyes.

"This can't all be my fault," he says.

"I know, I'm not saying it is, I'm just trying to explain why—"

"Why you fucked a stranger?" he says, glancing at her reflection. He watches her cheeks redden, tears well in her eyes.

"You were such hard work."

He barks a laugh. "I'm hard work. I don't argue, I clean up after myself, I fucking encourage you every time you go after a promotion at work, even if it means I don't see you for weeks while you work ridiculous hours."

"Yes." She exhales for a long time. "And that's how you float by. Remember when we first went out? The arguments we'd have, the ideas we'd discuss, the way we fucked?"

He does remember it. Familiar, and foreign. Like a place he can't find his way back to. He turns, tries to step past her. She blocks him.

"What I did was wrong. Horrible even. But it was a cry for help. Please, Adrian." She grabs his hands with hers, squeezes until they hurt. He can feel her pain, feel her anguish, her desire. "Please, come back to me. Fight for me. For the us that once was. Please?"

He stares into her eyes. Big, brown eyes. He can't remember the last time he looked into them. Saw how much lay behind them. The honesty. He opens his mouth to respond when a car horn sounds. Candice's head jerks around like she might be able to see the car through the walls of their house. Without eye contact, it's easier. He pulls his hands free. "That's my ride," he says.

"Your ride?"

He nods. "I'm sorry, Candice. I've got to go." He eases past her, moves quickly to the garage. She doesn't follow.

When he raises the garage door, Taylor is waiting, parked in his driveway, the back of her hatchback open. It's still light out, but not for much longer.

He carries the machine to her car, manoeuvres it into the back, closes the hatch. He climbs into the passenger seat, and Taylor reaches across, places a hand on his knee, squeezes.

"Ready?" she asks. He nods. She starts the car, eases out of the driveway.

As they gain speed, he turns and looks back at the house. He sees Candice standing in the open garage, watching. He watches her until they turn out of the street, until he can't see Candice or his house anymore.

Something has been set in motion. Something that he can't stop now even if he wanted to.

"Infinite Possibilities" continues in next month's issue.
See Parts I, II, and III of Michael Gardner's story "Infinite Possibilities" online at Metaphorosis.
If you liked it, leave a comment. Authors love that!
Remember to subscribe to our e-mail updates so you'll know when new stories are posted.

Copyright

Title information

Metaphorosis November 2022

ISSN: 2573-136X (online)
ISBN: 978-1-64076-240-4 (e-book)
ISBN: 978-1-64076-241-1 (paperback)

Publisher

Metaphorosis
a magazine of speculative fiction

Metaphorosis Magazine is an imprint of Metaphorosis Publishing
Neskowin, OR, USA

www.metaphorosis.com

"Metaphorosis" is a registered trademark.

Discounts available

Substantial discounts are available for educational institutions, including writing workshops. Discounts are also available for quantity purchases. For details, contact Metaphorosis at metaphorosis.com/about

Metaphorosis Publishing

Metaphorosis offers beautifully written science fiction and fantasy. Our imprints include:

Metaphorosis Magazine
Plant Based Press
Verdage
Vestige

You can also find us:
@MetaphorosisMag, @Metaphorosis
www.facebook.com/metaphorosis

Help keep Metaphorosis running by supporting us at
Patreon.com/metaphorosis

See more about some of our books on the following pages.

Metaphorosis Magazine

Metaphorosis
a magazine of speculative fiction

Metaphorosis is an online speculative fiction magazine dedicated to quality writing. We publish an original story every week, along with author bios, interviews, and notes on story origins.

We also publish monthly print and e-book issues, as well as yearly Best of and Complete anthologies.

Come and see us online at magazine.Metaphorosis.com.

Plant Based Press

plant
based
press

Vegan-friendly science fiction and fantasy, including anthologies of the year's best SFF stories, from 2016-2020.

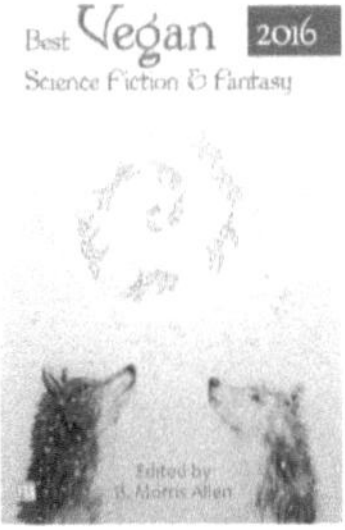

Best **Vegan** 2020
Science Fiction & Fantasy

Edited by
B. Morris Allen

Best **Vegan** 2019
Science Fiction & Fantasy

Edited by
B. Morris Allen

Best **Vegan** 2018
Science Fiction & Fantasy

Edited by
B. Morris Allen

Best **Vegan** 2017
Science Fiction & Fantasy

Edited by
B. Morris Allen

Best **Vegan** 2016
Science Fiction & Fantasy

Edited by
B. Morris Allen

Chambers of the Heart
speculative stories
by
B. Morris Allen

A heart that's a building, a dog that's a program, a woman sinking irretrievably — stories about love, loss, and movement.

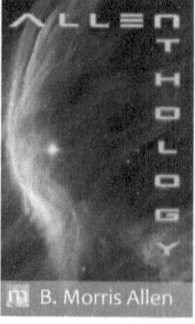

Susurrus

A darkly romantic story of magic, love, and suffering.

Allenthology: Volume I

Including three full collections of SFF stories.

Verdage

Science fiction and fantasy books for writers — full of great stories, often with an additional focus on the craft of speculative fiction writing.

Reading 5X5 x3

Changes

How do stories move from 'maybe' to published?

Here are 15 case studies of stories published in *Metaphorosis* magazine.

Reading 5X5 x2

Duets

How do authors' voices change when they collaborate?

A round-robin of five talented science fiction and fantasy authors collaborating with each other and writing solo.

Including stories by Evan Marcroft, David Gallay, J. Tynan Burke, L'Erin Ogle, and Douglas Anstruther.

Score

an SFF symphony

An anthology with an emotional score from the heights of joy to the depths of despair – but always with a little hope shining through.

Reading 5X5

Five stories, five times

See how different writers take on the same material.

Reading 5X5

Writers' Edition

Two extra stories, the story seed, and authors' notes on writing.

Vestige

Novelettes, novellas, and novels by Metaphorosis authors.

The Nocturnals
Mariah Montoya

Night is Dangerous.
Day is deadly.

Where day and night last thirty years, humans move constantly stay ahead of the night and cruel Nocturnals that call it home. But a boy is lost out there.